THE LAST CHANCE!

The woman was starting toward him, the shotgun pointed at his chest. Raider felt dangerously close to passing out. He shook and shook his head, trying to rid himself of the swimming fuzziness.

He staggered to his feet, fought off collapse as his head whirled, and stumbled forward. He was within ten strides of them when the woman, standing three lengths of the shotgun barrel from Steinbrenner, heard him and foolishly turned to look. Steinbrenner sprang at her, knocking her flat, the shotgun blowing the second barrel. Down he went, scrambling, retrieving his gun, crouching behind her, firing at Raider...

RAIDER

THE CHEYENNE FRAUD

BERKLEY BOOKS, NEW YORK

THE CHEYENNE FRAUD

A Berkley Book/published by arrangement with
the author

PRINTING HISTORY
Berkley edition/February 1988

ISBN: 0-425-10634-9

A BERKLEY BOOK ® TM 757,375
Berkley Books are published by the Berkley Publishing Group,
200 Madison Avenue, New York, NY 10016.
The name "BERKLEY" and the "B" logo
are trademarks belonging to the Berkley Publishing Corporation.

PRINTED IN THE UNITED STATES OF AMERICA

10 9 8 7 6 5 4 3 2 1

CHAPTER ONE

Allan Pinkerton's superintendent, operations manager, and right-hand man William Wagner had just become a father for the ninth time. Delia Pinkerton, wife of the chief's son Robert, was preparing to present Robert with their third child.

This sudden, seemingly uncontrollable epidemic of childbearing, combined with Raider's lingering and from all appearances incurable resentment over his former partner, Doc Weatherbee's defection, plunged the lean, rawhide tough, acid tongued, longtime Pinkerton operative into a morass of self-pity. His stubbled face was that of a man who had been chewing bitter pills, eating sour grapes, and sipping venom. He sat in his Levi's, disreputable wool shirt, and deerskin vest in Will Wagner's office puffing on the new father's gift of a La Mathilde cigar (50 to a box, price: $3.00) and ruminated glumly on the emptiness, loneliness, and pointlessness of his life.

"Why so down, Rade?" Wagner asked amiably.

"My dogs hurt. It's these Chicago sidewalks. They're hard as rails."

"Cheer up, you'll be leaving soon."

1

"Yeah, saddled with some furriner who can't speak English hardly none, don't know one end of a mount from the other, shoots with his eyes closed . . ."

He dropped his butt to the rug and flattened it with his heel. Wagner hastily retrieved it and, carrying it as he would a dead rodent, conveyed it to the ashtray on his desk.

"Come on, Rade, be fair. The chief's let you work without a partner for well over a year. In direct violation of his own rule book, as you well know. It seems to me the least you could do is accept this assignment gracefully. It's not forever. You could wrap things up in three weeks."

"This *sauerkrauter* savvy any English?"

"See here, you can stop that before you start. He's German, he's not a *sauerkrauter* or *Wienerschnitzeler* or anything else derogatory. And he speaks perfect English. Better than you."

"Ha."

"He's a thoroughgoing professional. The Berlin police force boasts just about the highest standards in Europe. He's been a *geheime Polizist* for—"

"A what?"

"Police detective."

"He talk like that?"

"You know what one of your biggest problems is? Your tendency to rip people to shreds before you even lay eyes on them."

"Makes sense. If they turn out okay I'm ahead o' the game, right?"

"I don't follow that at all."

The door opened. Allan Pinkerton, the dour, flint-dispositioned, frugal Scot; founder and chief of the Pinkerton National Detective Agency—"the eye that never sleeps"—introduced Police Detective Rudolph Fenstermacher. Raider rose from his chair and shook his outstretched hand as he appraised him. Rudolph was about his own age, slightly taller than his six-foot-two, blond, with the fair complexion that generally goes with the coloring. He was ruggedly built. His posture looked a trifle too stiff, as if his back were welded to a crowbar. His handsome face was divided horizontally by a set of magnificent mustachios terminating in points that poked upward sharply and looked so stiff they appeared lacquered. He was blessed with a disarming smile, one that instantly invited Raider to like him. Which, of course, annoyed the Pinkerton. The least of his desires at the moment was to be pleasantly surprised.

"Detective Fenstermacher is on the trail of a master counterfeiter, one—"

"Gerhard Steinbrenner."

The name was easily understood, his English so slightly accented Raider could dismiss it as no accent at all.

"He come to the States?" he asked.

"Nae!" boomed Pinkerton. "Whatever gives you thot idea? Fosh, mon, do you think Rudolph is o'er here sight-seeing?"

"I just asked, goddamn it!"

The chief dismissed this with a wave of his massive hand and a slight curling of his lip.

"Enough pleasantries, lods. Will, come into my office. We most go o'er this month's expenses. As usual they're scandalously high. At the rate our operatives in the field squander cash and cheat on their swindle sheets we'll be out of business and downstairs in the gutter in three weeks."

This last was aimed squarely at Raider, suggesting that he was the sole squanderer-cheater.

"We'll leave you two to get better acquainted. Rudolph, lod, kindly fill him in on the details."

Wagner buttoned his vest, stumped out his cigar, and followed his chief out. Rudy and Raider stood awkwardly eyeing each other in silence. The German was the first to break it.

"I understand that you have been working alone for the past few months," he said almost shyly.

"More'n a year now. My partner o' sixteen years up an' quit me cold. Straight outta the blue. Sorta puts ya in mind o' the rat desertin' the sinkin' ship. A woman, nat'rally;

turned his head from his sworn duty to bedroom dilly-dal-
lyin', moonlight mushery. . ."

"Moonlight mushery?"

Rudy whipped out a notebook and a small gold pencil
and noted down the phrase.

"I am collecting American slang expressions. The first
section is devoted to them. The second half to social expressions, what we call in the Fatherland *Idiomatische aus-
drücke*."

"Huh?"

"Moonlight mushery, that is good. But to return to business; I just wish you to know before we start that I appreciate your willingness to work with me. And I intend to
cooperate with you at every turn."

"You are? Hey, that's great. You know somethin'? You
speak real good English."

"Thank you, I studied it in college."

"College man, eh? Weatherbee was a college man. Har-
vard. He spoke it real good, too." Overcome by a sudden
surge of munificence, he reached into Wagner's box of
cigars and shoved four at Rudy. "Have a cigar, Rudy
partner."

"Thank you . . . partner."

He took one. Raider stuck the remaining three into his
own shirt pocket. Rudy smiled: part friendliness, part re-
lief, Raider assumed as he watched it spread across his
face. They were getting off on the right foot. It couldn't
hurt. Oh, he still resented Pinkerton's pairing him up with
a stranger, a foreigner to boot, but Wagner did have a
point: the chief *had* bent over backwards to accommodate
him for quite a time. He did owe him.

Rudy filled him in on Gerhard Steinbrenner. He was
enormously skilled in the arts of counterfeiting currency:
artist, engraver, printer, distributor; shrewd, patient, not at
all greedy in the manner of most counterfeiters, and pos-
sessed of an uncanny instinct that alerted him in the nick of
time every time the law began to close in.

"We get there and he has flown," said Rudy discouragedly. "It has been like that for three years now. I have come close a dozen times only to miss him."

Steinbrenner's success at eluding capture had heightened interest in apprehending him to the point where he had finally decided that fleeing the Continent would be in his best interest. Like the relentless Jobert pursuing Jean Valjean in Hugo's *Les Misérables,* however, Rudy refused to renounce the chase.

"Another secret of his success is his positive *Wähnsinn,* ah, how do you say it, mania for preparedness. He formulates his plan and sticks to it through thick and thin."

"You're sure he came to the States?"

"He was seen by a customs man when he landed in New York. The New York office of your agency was informed."

"That'd be George Bangs. So you must know what this Steinwhatever looks like."

"About my height, dark hair, eyes as black as coal, mustache, Vandyke beard . . ."

"How old?"

"That is hard to say. But make no mistake, he is here. And our informant, a former ladyfriend in Berlin, claims he is heading for Cheyenne in Wyoming."

"Ain't it always the way: a woman scorned is always the first to get to the whistle an' blow it."

Again Rudy whipped out his notebook and wrote, but stopped abruptly and looked up. "Meaning?"

"Snitch. A stool pigeon."

"Ah, *wunderbar.*"

"Sure does narrow it down, I mean if it does turn out he's headin' for Cheyenne."

"You know Cheyenne?"

"Like the back o' my hand. It's good as my home town. Nice town; a little hairy after sundown, but show me a town out west that ain't and it's gotta be every house a church. You drink?" Again Rudy smiled. "Then you'll like Cheyenne. Rail town. Union Pacific. Up an' comin place."

"Are there red Indians there?"

"There's red Injuns evvywhere, 'cept here. In Chicago's mostly micks an' *krauteaters,* polacks . . ."

"Kraut?"

"'Scuse me, Germans. Hey, I'm hungry, whatta ya say we strap on the feed bag? I mean eat some food."

Raider's invitation to lunch was carefully phrased so as not to give the impression that he was "taking" Rudy to lunch and was prepared to pick up the check. They walked to the Union Restaurant on Randolph Street. Raider's garb, his stubble, and his Stetson raised not a few eyebrows on the way to their table. It was getting on to one o'clock, and the early arrivals in the noonday crowd had finished their lunch, opening up places for latecomers. They'd gotten there at the best possible time.

After they had both finished their chops and peas, Raider turned to Rudy. "Mmmmm. You ride a horse?"

"Yes, but not a western saddle; rather what we in the Fatherland call a military seat."

"Cavalry dishpan. No, no, no, don't put that in your notebook. Chrissakes, you'll fill it up before we get to Omaha the rate you're goin'. You pack a gun?"

"My service revolver. A Gruener. They do not manufacture them anymore. It is not the most accurate weapon, but it is comfortable in my hand, I like it. It has seen me through many a close call."

"On the job."

"No, I mean during the war. The Franco-Prussian War."

"You fought?"

"I was an officer."

He unbuttoned his shirt. Affixed to his long johns were the Prussian Iron Cross and two other medals.

"Oh for Chrissakes . . ."

"Excuse me?"

"Nothin'. You musta been some kinda hero. You know how to use a rifle?"

"I never have. My pistol serves me admirably."

"Yeah, only long range it's about as useful as a extra toe. Time's wastin'. We'd better get packed and see about catching a train." He laid some money on the table.

Rudy eyed it questioningly. "Is that enough, do you think?"

"Plenty for my half. Plus the tip, o' course. I come here all the time when I'm in town on account the service is the best as you can see. I always leave a extra dime for the tip."

CHAPTER TWO

First impressions can lead one into leaping to wrong conclusions about a person. Rudy and Raider got off on the right foot, but a little stumbling was to follow. Rudy was not quite the paragon of cooperation he announced he intended to be. He had a stubborn streak; he was finicky, incredibly, even infuriatingly meticulous in his attention to his mustachios. He boasted that every morning upon arising, wherever he was, whatever the press of time, he allotted at least thirty minutes preparing his pride and joy for the day: trimming, combing, brushing, waxing, and sharpening the tips until they resembled blond darts. He hauled out notebook and pencil on average four times an hour, or so it seemed to Raider. Raider decided it would be best if he helped him fill it in short order, then hopefully he'd put it away until the case was wrapped up. Of course he could always buy a second notebook when the first one was filled. Nevertheless, Raider inundated him with slang: "savvy," "rotgut," "salty dog," "fumadiddle," "faradiddle," and the like. As for his collection of western social expressions, designed to impress the ladies and dignified by some semblance of gentility, "my little prairie flower," "sweeter than a honeybee's crop," "conversation fluid" for "rotgut," "nominate your poison" for "what will you have to drink," etc. got him off to a good start.

They would travel from Chicago to Omaha and there change trains to cross Nebraska and the Wyoming border to Cheyenne. The total distance was approximately a thousand miles, and with scheduled stops and unforeseen delays, would consume more than a day and a half, Raider figured. They boarded at the La Salle Street Station at ten past seven and went to sleep in their seats around eleven. That is, Rudy went to sleep. Raider and the other occupants of the car tried; all but a few, seated a safe distance from Rudy and Raider, found sleep impossible.

Rudy snored. That is to say bellowed in his sleep: roared, carried on like April thunder, a train whistle in a small room, a sawmill. He snored louder than an overcrowded bunkhouse, Raider concluded barely fifteen seconds into his performance. It was a wonder he didn't shatter the window beside which he slouched. Passengers seated around them chorused protest.

Raider elbowed him awake. "Chrissakes, man, do you have to snore like that? You're bustin' everybody's eardrums."

"Put a cork in it," suggested an overdressed young man seated opposite.

"Tie a hanky under your nose," offered a woman behind them.

"Move on into the next car, why don'cha?" said another man.

Rudy apologized, went back to sleep, and resumed the onslaught—if anything, even louder than before. People got their bags and belongings down from the overhead racks and left the car muttering and complaining. Presently only a handful of passengers remained. Raider finally gave up himself, wandering to the front end of the car and out into the vestibule. He lay down on the plate steel step top and, using his saddlebags for a pillow, fell asleep.

Rudy woke him the next morning. He admitted he'd been up an hour and felt marvelous after his night's sleep.

He also admitted that he had monopolized the necessary mirror for half an hour, much to the chagrin of the other passengers. But his mustachios looked magnificent. His popularity, however, was in rapid decline, and when the two of them returned to their seat they ran a gauntlet of grouchy and threatening glares. Raider refrained from comment, knowing they weren't directed at him. If Rudy noticed he gave no sign.

They reached Omaha at 10:20 A.M. The conductor announced that all through passengers to North Platte and points beyond would be obliged to change trains and that the westbound train would be departing at noon sharp on track 21.

They dallied at the lunch counter in the depot, sipping Sultana coffee and eating doughnuts. Rudy took a pill.

"What's that for?" Raider asked pointedly.

"Iron. for energy. It keeps me at peak strength."

"You don't look like you need any o' that."

Rudy showed him the bottle. "Haunschweiger's Blut Stärkener. How do you say it? Invigorator."

"Whatever."

"Try one."

"No thanks. If my blood gets any stronger it's liable to bust outta my veins."

Rudy sipped and set his cup down. "About my snoring," he said sheepishly. "Again I apologize. I know it is unusually loud. I have had many complaints. I have seen many doctors, but there is no cure. In the army they made me sleep alone. When we get to Cheyenne perhaps it would be best if we have separate accommodations."

"Separate hotels, maybe."

"I am sorry if I inconvenienced you, partner."

"Forget it, I've slept in worse places than train vestibules. Chrissakes, I've slept in trees. I just hope for your sake you don't go blowin' pieces o' your throat out your nose."

Rudy got out a watch the size of a tomato. "It is fifteen minutes and eight seconds before noon. Time to board."

"Wait'll ten of or so. No sense sittin' an' fidgetin'."

"But I always allow exactly fourteen minutes before boarding a train. One must be methodical about such things, don't you think? As punctual as the railroad."

"Oh hell, I don't care. If you wanna."

They paid separately, Rudy noting down the expense in a second notebook. Raider pictured his pockets filled with notebooks.

"Do you not keep a record of your expenditures?" Rudy asked.

"Sure. In my head. Rough estimate. I mean ol' A.P. knows how much is reasonable to spend from Chicago to Cheyenne. The big expense is the ticket, and with our U.P. passes we don't have to spring for that."

"Nevertheless, I find it best to keep a precise record. Come, come, come!"

He hurried off. Raider sighed and followed him at a saunter. Why, he wondered, did everyone he met have to be so riddled with imperfections and shortcomings? Why couldn't folks be as even-tempered, agreeable, easy going, good-hearted, gracious, generous, likable, personable, and popular as he was. It was a mystery; he couldn't figure it out.

There were only four stops to North Platte and no stops from there to Cheyenne, two hundred and forty miles and six and a quarter hours beyond. They left North Platte shortly after 7:00 P.M. A butcher had boarded and was dispensing sandwiches and raspberry crush. They bought two roast beef sandwiches apiece, Rudy noting the expense down in his book. All the way from Omaha he had been regaling Raider with stories about his experiences in the war. By the time they left North Platte Raider was beginning to feel as if he'd fought with him side by side.

Happily, Rudy changed the subject.

"Do you not think there are a great many workers on this train?"

"Well, did you notice when the conductor came by that young buck with him? The older fella's trainin' him. Showin' him the ropes. That's what they do on the U.P., train the young fellas breakin' in right on the job. So what we got here is double the usual crew an' maybe even more."

"I see. In the Fatherland the railroad personnel are trained in schools."

"Yeah, but this is on the job. Makes a lotta sense, don't it?"

"It does."

It did make sense. It was almost profoundly logical to Raider, despite the fact that he was making it all up solely to keep the conversation away from the Franco-Prussian War. Unfortunately, as on target as his explanation may have sounded, he was dead wrong. Two minutes later the train shuddered to a stop in the middle of nowhere and the conductor and his apprentice at one end, and a trainman and his at the other, pulled guns and held up the passengers.

"Sonovabitch!" burst out Raider as a woman screamed, a man shouted, and three or four others cursed. The holdup man at the far end fired a shot through the roof. Silence settled instantaneously on the passengers.

"You're on, folks. Show's all yours. Dig down deep and come up with everything and nobody gets hurt. We'll be outta here in five minutes tops and you'll be on your merry way."

Two of them produced flour sacks, holding them open.

"I cannot, I will not give them my watch," muttered Rudy.

"You better. You make 'em take it off ya and they might take your life right along with it. You don't argue with a hostile iron in these parts."

"It was my father's and his father's before him. It is an antique Perrelet automatic winding watch. His invention. It is priceless. And the sentimental value . . ."

"Hand it over. You'll get it back."

"How?"

"The second they're out the door, we'll go after them. Look out the window. You don't see no horseflesh out there, do you?"

No sooner did he say it than the sound of galloping

reached their ears. Through a stand of cottonwood two riders could be seen leading at least twenty horses.

"Shit," muttered Raider. "Whatta you need with a watch anyhow? You can always tell time by the stars."

"In the sack, brother," said the "apprentice conductor," shoving it so close to Raider's scowl one would have imagined he was about to hang a nosebag full of oats on a city horse. Raider intensified his scowl, sighed, and dropped in thirty dollars paper and his change.

"Your watch, too," said the man, leering.

Close up he wasn't nearly as young as Raider had first thought; he had a weasel face, slender-muzzled and beady-eyed. Mean-looking, and had obviously been around the barn with his sack and six-shooter.

"I got no watch. Don't carry none. Search me if you don't believe me."

"If I do and I find one you're dead."

"Go ahead, search."

"I believe you. You, Mr. Mustache, cough up your cash and valuables. That chain there says *you* pack a watch. Let's have—"

It was as far as he got. Up came Rudy's right hand filled with gun. The single shot blew the man into the lap of the overdressed young fellow across the aisle. All hell erupted. Two of the holdup men got a bead on Rudy and commenced firing. Everybody hit the floor.

"What the hell you do that for?" rasped Raider, down on hands and knees and partway under the seat.

"I told you my watch is priceless."

"So's my ass! Chrissakes, isn't yours? They'll blow you fulla daylight now. They'll hafta piece you together like a busted vase before they can bury you. You gotta be loco."

"Loco?"

"Crazy, man, boss-simple, lame-headed . . ."

"Ahhhh, *wunderbar*!" He thrust his hand inside his jacket after his notebook.

Raider pulled his arm away angrily. "Not now, damn it!"

He got out his Peacemaker, whirled the cylinder, and

sneaked a look around the end of the seat. He drew two slugs too close for his trouble, coming from the rear of the car.

"Jesus!"

"They should have hit you," said Rudy casually, all but yawning. "They are close enough. They are not good shots."

This said, he jumped up and jerked down, getting off two shots of his own between the two moves. A loud scrambling could be heard at the opposite end. Raider risked another look. The two holdup men at the rear lay dead, their smoking pistols in their hands. The two at the opposite end had taken one look and were getting out. Rudy stood up, ran a finger up to the point of one end of his mustachios, then the other, blew the smoke from the muzzle of his Gruener, and turned on his most ingratiating smile. Outside, the members of the gang, having cleaned out their respective cars, were hightailing it for the horses brought up and waiting in the trees. Raider jammed a boot through the window and began blasting. Rudy joined him. Other passengers took up the attack. The surviving outlaws mounted up and barreled away.

A passing breeze curled through the cottonwoods. Raider counted six dead sprawled on the ground; two more jerked and joined them as he took in the grisly scene. A cheer went up, reverberating from one end of the car to the other. The passengers still on the floor had risen as one and rushed toward them. They surrounded Rudy, pumped his hand, slapped him on the back, congratulated him effusively. Two women kissed him on the cheek.

Raider bent over the dead holdup man across the aisle and retrieved his thirty dollars and change.

Rudy, he thought. Rudolph Fensterwhatever. Son of a bitch could shoot. And was cool as a riverboat gambler under fire. It promised an interesting assignment.

Twenty minutes later the train resumed its run to the border and across it toward Cheyenne minus conductors, trainmen, and apprentices. Fortunately for all on board the outlaws had not replaced the engineer and fireman. Raider speculated on what had happened to the rest of the crew; he pictured them bound and gagged and fuming in the dark corner of an unused shed somewhere in the Omaha yards.

"Good job, Rudy," he said. "Though I gotta admit I figgered you went haywire there for a shake or two. Shook me up for fair."

"Haywire?" Out came the notebook and pencil. He eyed Raider questioningly.

"Off your rocker."

"Off . . .?"

"Never mind, never mind. Chrissakes, isn't that thing full up yet?"

"Almost, but do not worry, I have with me four more." He licked the point of his pencil. "Hay . . . wi . . . re . . ."

CHAPTER THREE

Cheyenne had mushroomed since Raider's last visit three years before. It had become the cow capital of the northern ranges, although it could hardly compare with the cow towns of Kansas. Hairy it may have been after dark, but there are degrees of wildness, and compared to Abilene, Dodge City, and Ellsworth, it came dangerously close to downright genteel.

Rudy carried two huge grain leather Gladstone bags. Two minutes away from the depot he spotted a "For Rent" sign with "Inquire next door" inscribed below. The sign was nailed to a veranda pillar of a small house lodged between two large commercial buildings.

"That is for me, partner," he crowed.

"It's gonna cost you four times as much as a hotel room," said Raider. "I mean we could bunk on separate floors," he added hastily.

"No. I prefer my own place. It would be terribly embarrassing to take a hotel room and be thrown out in the middle of the night for disturbing the other guests."

The house rented for six dollars a week. Raider considered the price outrageous and said so. Rudy dismissed it as a necessary expense, noting it down in his little book after accepting the key from the real estate broker in the office in the building next door. Rudy also invested in a whipped-brim Dakota Stetson. It fit, but it made his mustachios look even more out of place, Raider thought, but he made no comment. Rudy also purchased a rugged little mustang and well-used Texas saddle, it being the closest he could come in style and proportions to a military dishpan. He was a little concerned about the pommel. He'd never ridden a horse with a saddle with an apple.

"Will it hurt me in my . . . my sensitive area if the horse stops short, do you think?"

"Hell no," Raider assured him. "Long as you keep hold of it an' your feet in your stirrups. If you gotta stop fast and you think it's gonna jam your jewels, just rise up over it a mite, just enough to clear it. If you get up too high and she brakes sudden-like, you'll go ass over teakettle."

He himself rented a little roan mare and western rig. He fleetingly considered investing in a Winchester, but decided to put it off until if and when it might be needed. He helped Rudy get settled, then went across the street to the Cheyenne House and got a single room. "The cheapest we got, mister," according to the clerk.

"Great."

The walls and ceiling were a mass of water stains, the washbowl was cracked in four places, the mirror foggy, the two-inch-thick tick mattress crunched loudly when he tested it and promised all the comfort of hardscrabble under the stars. The pillow was a rock, the linens yellow with age or something. All in all it looked to be all the comforts of home. He found it perfectly satisfactory.

He rejoined Rudy at the bar in the Pioneer Saloon four doors down the street. He ordered a tumbler of Hofstetter's Rye.

Rudy asked for beer. One taste and his favorite smile vanished, displaced by a look bordering on fear. "This is not German beer."

"This is not Germany."

They put their heads together and discussed the situation

in whispers. They agreed that rather than go out looking for Steinbrenner they would be better off checking around town discreetly in quest of counterfeit bills. If they came across anyone stuck with one they could trace it back to its source.

"Hopefully," said Raider.

"I like it," said Rudy. "It will enable us to, so to speak, sneak up on him without his being aware. And possibly avoid bloodshed."

"Right. There's only one fly in the ointment. He coulda come, hung his paper, all he planned on passin' out, and already left town. Counterfeiters operate that way, you know. Pull their scam and move on."

"He cannot have been here more than three or four days. My guess is he is still around. This beer is foul. It tastes like the liquid that sits at the top of a new jar of mustard. Wretched."

He ordered a glass of Hofstetter's, more to rid his mouth of the taste of the beer than for enjoyment. They drank themselves into a mellow state, found the nearest diner, enjoyed a late supper, and parted company in front of Rudy's house, planning to breakfast together at eight sharp the following morning and start to work.

Raider strolled across the street to the Cheyenne House. He did not notice the expensively dressed, heavily upper-decked, pretty young thing sailing along the sidewalk at right angles to him until he reached the sidewalk himself. Head down, deeply immersed in thoughts of Rudy and the case, he bumped into her and knocked her tumbling.

"Why don't you watch where you're going, cowboy!" she snapped.

He offered a hand to help her up. She waved it away, but the billowing fullness of her taffeta skirt made it difficult for her to get up on her own, and he finally had to help her to her feet.

"I'm sorry, I'm sorry. I just didn't see you. I had my head down, thinkin' about the funeral."

"Funeral?"

"Ma. Poor soul. To be struck down so sudden-like. In

her prime. She was all the family I had left. My two brothers died in the war, you know. My pa was taken with pneumonia two winters back."

The exasperation drained from her face. She cocked her head and eyed him sympathetically. "I'm so sorry, I didn't realize . . . Of course it was an accident."

"No, no, no, I shoulda watched where I was goin'."

"No harm done, really."

"Lucky it's dry out and you didn't get mud on your skirts there. My, what a pretty outfit. You sure enough got taste in duds."

Her eyes said she was feeling a surge of warm, good feeling toward him, though it was impossible to return the compliment. She *was* pretty, he noted. Her eyes were large and dark, her complexion flawless, skin delicately soft, so soft he felt the urge to reach out and caress it. But it was her mouth that caught and held his attention. It was sensuously full, her lips gleaming in the doorlight of the hotel. And the way she displayed it, open just a slit. She moved her lips, closing them, opening them and pushing the tip of her tongue against the upper one.

His gaze slowly descended to her massive breasts. She was suddenly breathing heavily and faster. He swallowed and smiled. She acknowledged it with her own.

"You staying here?" she asked in a low, sultry tone.

"Mmmmm."

"Me too. Room four-B. Up the stairs and to your right."

"Four-B."

"Four-B. I'm only here a few days. Don't know a blessed soul."

"I don't myself."

"It's so lonesome, especially at night."

"It is."

"I . . . I hope you don't think I'm being forward, but I'm dying for someone to talk to."

"Me too."

"Why don't you drop up and we can chat."

"That'd be real nice."

"Give me five minutes, then come on up, okay?"

"It'd be a pleasure."

"Oh, it will be. Four-B."

"Four-B."

He ran out of patience after four minutes by the clock behind the front desk. Four minutes proved adequate. When he knocked softly on her door and she opened it his jaw dropped, his heart thundered to life in his chest at the sight, and he swallowed so hard it hurt.

And he fell in love.

"Come in, come in, what a pleasant surprise. I really was afraid you'd think I was being much too forward."

A half hour later, the deed accomplished to their mutual satisfaction, she sat up in the bed and shook him awake from his dozing. "That'll be five bucks."

"Five! That's highway robbery! I'll give you a buck four bits."

"Four-fifty."

A knock sounded. "Imogene?" called a muffled voice.

"Damn. Okay, okay, give me the buck and a half, get your clothes on, and get out of here."

"With friggin' pleasure."

He hauled on his drawers, half buttoned his shirt, armed into his vest, and toed on his boots. By which time the knocker was practically battering the door in his impatience. Raider jerked it open. There stood a young giant behind a black-as-pitch beard that reached his belt buckle. Behind him stood another man. Behind *him* a third. A total of seven made up the line stretching down the hallway. Eight, as another appeared at the top of the stairs. Raider turned back to her and scowled accusingly.

"Disgustin'! You oughta be ashamed o' yourself."

"What should you be, proud? Get out of here. Next!"

He lay in bed thinking about Rudy and tomorrow. He had to concede that Mr. Mustache was certainly holding up his end of the partnership;—at least up to now. Being German, Raider had expected he'd be much more pigheaded. Of course, they had yet to arrive at their first real disagreement on anything. Still, when Raider suggested they canvas the town in quest of funny money rather than go hunting for Steinwhatever, Rudy had jumped at the idea. He was being almost too cooperative. He recalled Rudy's description of the culprit in Wagner's office. Dark hair, dark eyes and well-built was practically it. Pretty vague, but it at least cut out everybody with blond hair and red hair. If they succeeded in tracking just one phony bill to its source and that source turned out to be an individual of such a description they'd be in great shape.

Was Rudy being overly cooperative? Was there such a thing? Or was it that Raider had become so accustomed to arguing over practically every move they made, every tactic, every decision with Weatherbee—not to mention everybody else the chief had paired him with since Weatherbee's defection and before he relented and let him go out on his own.

Weatherbee. Did Doc miss him as much as he missed Doc? Probably not, not with his wife to hold his hand, and his job, and the high-society whirl. He was living a full life, and a gilt-edged one. Of course the absence of excitement had to make it dull as a stagnant puddle. No danger, no risks, no gunplay, nothing but linen tablecloths, clean silverware, the country club, the governor's ball, charity to- dos every other week, champagne, and $100 suits.

"What the hell kinda life is that? Really. I wouldn't swap saddles with the sonovabitch for all the tea in China *and* Japan. Man's a damn fool to get married. Ring through the nose, anvil round the neck, hobbles on his ankles."

A knock sounded.

"Yeah?"

"Imogene?" asked a male voice tentatively.

"Upstairs. Four-B, goddamn it!"

CHAPTER FOUR

They made the rounds of the local banks looking for bogus money. They paused on the sidewalk coming out of the Cattleman's Bank on Main Street. Each of them lit up one of William Wagner's La Mathildes.

"You know somethin', I never used to smoke," said Raider. "I took it up after Weatherbee deserted me. He used to suck on Ol' Virginia cheroots. Kid stuff. Tasted like shoelaces. Now this here's a real smoke, a man's smoke."

"Did you take it up to remind you of him?" Rudy asked.

"Oh hell no!"

So abrupt and so emphatic was his denial it was obvious that this was precisely the reason.

"I can see I am stepping into large shoes," continued Rudy. "He must have been a first-rate operative."

"He was okay. Long as I was around to keep him straight and bail him outta trouble, outta fracases an' such. Woulda been doomed on his own. We're not having much luck, are we?"

"Patience. How many more banks are there?"

"Just one. Farmers an' Merchants over on Fifth Street. About four blocks."

Gliding toward them was Cheyenne's most popular companion of the night, stunningly arrayed in a lavender silk ensemble, complete with parasol and pearl-studded white lace gloves. Raider looked and looked away, sending a hand up to his cheek to cover his profile. She passed with her nose in the air and followed her ample bosom toward the corner.

"Fine figure of a woman," commented Rudy.

"Two-bit whore for sure. Whores all the time dress to the hilt, you know. They should—they make money hand over fist. Like they say, a disgustin' necessary evil."

"As lovely from this angle as from the opposite," commented Rudy, following her with admiring eyes.

"They practice that twitch, you know. They got all kinda tricks down pat to entice the gullible, unwary, an' hard up. Disgustin'! There oughta be a law."

They had no luck at the Farmers and Merchants Bank. They visited stores and other places of business all over town, questioning clerks, secretaries, and other workers. No counterfeit money had turned up. Not a penny, much less a twenty, a fifty, or a hundred-dollar bill. They shared a table and a bottle of Ruckus Juice at the Pioneer.

"It is just possible that we actually beat him to town," said Rudy.

"Let's hope it's that. How far ahead of you was he when you landed in New York, do you figger?"

"I can only guess, but no more than four or five days."

"Hey, he coulda stayed there and took it easy for a spell. You know, to rest up before he launches his big operation. Think about it: he's three thousand miles from home, he's gotta feel safe as a baby milkin' its ma, confident nobody's followin' him. His time is his own. Why rush all the way out here?"

"That is possible."

He didn't sound as if he wholeheartedly agreed.

Raider pressed him. "You did say he was patient as Job."

"Yes. I think we have to be also."

"You mean squat and wait for him?"

"I do not see what else we can do? Do you?"

"Well, it sure don't make much sense walkin' round buggin' the bankers an' merchants over an' over every day. They'll get sick of the sight of us."

"They know we are in town, where we can be reached if any counterfeit money does turn up."

"Hows about we give 'em three days. If by then we don't hear from any, we'll make the rounds again. It's possible the workmanship's so good it can't be spotted."

"If after we make inquiries the second time we still have no success, perhaps we never will. Perhaps he has changed his mind about coming here, and we will have to look elsewhere."

"Elsewhere's one helluva big territory out here. Cross your fingers it don't come to that."

"One other thing that I have been thinking about. We have not talked to the sheriff. Should we not take him into our confidence?"

"Plenty of time for that. If his nibs don't show up here, no point in talkin' to the law. If and when he does we can."

The self-imposed three-day waiting period put Raider on pins and needles. Inactivity always irritated him. To chase, shoot it out, win the day, and collar the miscreants was the name of his game and when he couldn't play or had to dally until he could it galled him. Rudy, on the other hand, turned out to be the soul of patience. He also found a better way to pass the time than loitering about and doing nothing other than eating, drinking, and sleeping. Over the three-day period the two went their separate ways, but Raider spied Rudy no fewer than six times. On each occasion Rudy was either going into or coming out of his rented house. Each time with a different girl on his arm. Each one better-looking than the previous one.

"Must be those foolish-lookin' mustaches crowdin' his face. Women do go gaga over the silliest damn things."

It was also plain that Rudy packed a rubber wallet. He had evidently arrived in the States loaded.

On a Thursday morning, four days after coming to town, they again met and set forth on their rounds. On the way to the Cattleman's Bank, the first stop on the route Raider had set out for them, Rudy stopped off at a notions store to pick up a bar of Reilly's Pomatum Mustaches Wax. Raider lingered outside, digging his breakfast out of his teeth with a kitchen match and people watching. Suddenly, what sounded like a full-scale melee erupted inside.

"Gimme my money, you dang swivel dude! Give it here or I'll blow your head off!"

In rushed Raider. The storekeeper behind the counter, clad in vest and shirtsleeves, looked apoplectic. His own unwaxed mustache flourished wildly left and right of his round, red, generous nose. He held an ancient Navy Colt in both trembling hands—aimed squarely at Rudy, standing less than a foot from the muzzle on the opposite side of the counter. Rudy's head was down. He held a magnifying glass. He was studiously examining a twenty-dollar bill, ignoring both man and Colt.

"What the hell's going' on!" exclaimed Raider.

"Him! He comes sashayin' in here askin' to buy mustache wax. I give it to him an' when he gives me the money and I open the till to give him his change, he snatches that twenny-dollar bill out of the drawer. Give it here, you!"

"It is counterfeit," said Rudy mildly, still not looking up. "Come and see, Raider."

"You're crazy in the dang head!" bawled the man. "That bill's good as gold. You gonna give it back or do I have to kill you to get it?"

"Calm down," said Raider. "Put away the cannon. Nobody's gonna steal nothin'."

"Just hand it over and get out, the both o' you!"

"Look," said Rudy to Raider, still not deigning to so

much as lift his attention from the glass and respond to the man behind the gun. Raider got the feeling that Rudy's ignoring him and his threats was annoying him even more than his refusal to return the money.

"Ellie Mae!" rasped the storekeeper to a frightened-looking little teenager behind the counter at the rear. "You mind the store. Keep your eyes on these two. I'm gettin' Mace Tunstall!"

So saying he jerked up the counter board, ran out into the street, and emptied his gun into the sky. A crowd quickly began to collect.

"What's he so antsy for?" Raider asked the girl. "Nobody's stealin' nothin'. We're Pinkerton detectives. We're in town lookin' for phony money. We were in here three days back. You were here, don'cha remember?"

She too obviously didn't care to try to remember. She was shaking like an aspen, her eyes saucering, teeth chattering.

"Calm down," said Raider.

"Look!"

Raider bent and peered through the magnifying glass.

"I don't see nothin' strange."

"Look at the flaws, the breaks in the lines. Look at the streaks of ink bridging the clear spaces. Some points are dull. Look there. Those faint ridges and hollows there and there. Have you a twenty? I have only small bills and larger ones."

"I got one, but there's no sense comparin' 'em."

"Let me have it."

"That bill's genuine."

"It cannot possibly be, not with such sloppy engraving. Give me yours."

Raider handed him his twenty.

Rudy held his breath as he compared them. "Ah-hah!"

"What?"

"Never mind the little flaws, look at the treasury seal. On your bill it is perfectly centered under the capital 'I' and 'N' in the word 'coin'. On this bill it is lower and slightly to the left. Definitely counterfeit. Unquestionably!"

"That don't prove beans. That treasury seal is all over the place on a twenty, on all bills. Government printers don't care about placin' it perfect, just as long as it's on there. An' all the other little flaws, look close an' you'll see 'em on both."

"Wait, wait."

Rudy compared the borders on both bills, Garfield's hair, and other complicated and intricately wrought areas. Looking at his face, Raider could see his enthusiasm seep slowly out of him.

"Gott in Himmel, you are right," he murmured. "What sloppy workmanship. What carelessness. German paper money is perfectly engraved, every line, every flourish, every shading; every hundred-mark note precisely like its fellows, and that is so with every denomination. Identical under the most powerful magnification."

"Just in case you forgot, this is America. Me and Weatherbee had a case back when down to Deming and Albuquerque, all over south New Mexico. Counterfeiter was with a travelin' carnival: the Great Zemo; the whole show did the distributin'. I got to know more about counterfeitin' on that one case that you could shake a stick at. And months after it was wrapped up I got to talkin' with a retired federal government engraver from the San Francisco mint. He give me an earful about the points an' the hollows an' breaks an' the way the Great Seal floats all over the word 'twenty'."

The crowd outside was becoming large. A tall, heavyset man came barging in followed by the storekeeper and a dozen rubberneckers. No sooner did the first two pass over the sill than the newcomer turned and barked the others back outside. He wore twin ivory-handled .45s, a silver buckle on his belt six inches square, and a gleaming five-point star with "SHERIFF" arcing across its face. He hadn't shaved in a week, and his stubble stuck forth from his cheeks and chin like thin black nails driven out from inside. He looked tough as a goat to Raider, and his hands, now moving to and sitting on his grips, looked like he could twist a bull's head clean off its neck.

"What do you think you're doing, you two?"

"That one there pinched my twenty, Mace," sputtered the storekeeper.

"I did not pinch anything, Sheriff."

Raider explained and dug out his Pinkerton I.D.

"We've got no counterfeit money in town," said Tunstall. "Is that twenty bogus?"

"It's good as gold," muttered Raider.

"See? I tolja, I tolja!" snapped the storekeeper, shoving his red face and redder nose up uncomfortably close to Rudy's.

"Give him back his money and let's go over to the office and sort this out," said Tunstall.

They started out.

Rudy stopped short. "I did not get my change for the twenty-five cents I gave him for the wax. It was only eight cents."

Standing just inside the door was a rack filled with shaving necessities. Raider took two more bars of Reilly's Pomatum and stuffed them in Rudy's pocket.

"Three times eight is twenty-four," he called back to the storekeeper. "You can keep the odd penny for your trouble."

"If either of you ever show your faces in here again, I'll blow your heads off!"

"He's never fired that thing in his entire life," murmured the sheriff.

The sheriff's office was typical, only the cells were not located in the rear with access by way of a door between, but in a separate building next door. Tunstall's lair boasted one amenity Raider could not recall seeing in any other sheriff's office he had ever been in: a carpet. A well-worn imitation Turkish carpet. The Neale & Urban safe, the door decorated with a mole's-eye view of the Rockies, supported the bulk of the sheriff's record. A small bookcase contained his law books and case files.

Pasteboard boxes were piled four high atop it. Other boxes crammed with folders and records filled the remainder of the space. The cheap walnut curtain-top desk pigeonholes were stuffed with correspondence and reports; the very top of the desk was piled with more papers. If there was a blotter gracing the working area it was well hidden by clutter. A Sholes typewriter sat on a small square table at one end of the desk. On the wall was a "Hayes for President" poster, a map of the U.S. so old and worn it had passed the yellowing age and was entering brown. There was also a calendar advertising the services of the Mohawk Fire Insurance Company.

There was only one chair, the sheriff's, a round back and dowel swivel chair, its legs bowing outward and bending back inward before reaching the floor. It looked like the manipulable claw that descends in a candy-toy grab machine in a penny arcade. Tunstall provided Raider and Rudy with stools.

"You could have checked in with me when you first hit town, you know," he said in a slightly offended tone. "It's just possible I could have saved you time and trouble. I know one thing: there hasn't been so much as a counterfeit single passed in this town in the seven years I've been sheriff. If there were, whoever it was passed to would come running to me."

"Providing they recognized it as counterfeit," said Rudy.

Raider nodded. "There's counterfeit and there's counterfeit, Sheriff. Some of it is so good it passes for months and months. It takes a sharp-eyed teller to spot trouble, and usually they're so busy pushin' bills back and forth through their hands, they don't get a chance to look close."

"This Steinbrenner is a master," continued Rudy. "There are engravers who turn out superb work but do not possess either the criminal cunning or the daring he boasts. There are criminals who are clever and immensely capable who could pass counterfeit currency with ease but do not have access to a superior product.

He is both in one. He has ravaged Europe—Berlin, Munich, Amsterdam, Antwerp, Brussels, even London. Now he is here."

"You sure?"

"Definitely."

"Why would he come all the way out here and bypass the big cities in the East?"

"Good question," Raider said to Rudy.

"I think the answer is that unlike Europe, where he is familiar with practically every nation, nearly every language, the U.S. represents a vast new arena to him. A truly foreign country. Unsure ground, so to speak. He knows the language, but not the people, not their ways. In every respect it is alien to him. Out here, with all due respect, Sheriff, law and order are not as—"

"As tight, as professional," interrupted Tunstall. "I know. You're right. I myself have the whole of Laramie County to cover. I could use twenty more men, but there just isn't the money in the budget. We're still a territory and likely will be for the next twenty or thirty years. But you've answered my question. I—"

The door burst open, slamming against the wall, jarring the calendar to an awkward angle. In flew a squat, bald-pated, flustered, and furious individual in his sixties, dressed to the hilt from his silk string tie down to spats and highly polished low calf-leather shoes.

"Sheriff! Sheriff! Look! Look!"

He held up a ten-dollar silver certificate, Robert Morris's aristocratic and slightly haughty face appraising the world out of his oval frame.

"It's a phony."

Tunstall gasped and practically snatched it from him. All four crowded around the desk as he shoved the clutter left and right and spread it to examine it. Rudy got out his magnifying glass.

"He's right," said Raider. "You can see without the glass. Look at the markin' in the upper-right corner." He pressed the corner between thumb and forefinger. Stuck to his thumb was what looked like pepper; on the corner he had pressed, salt. "It's the ink. It breaks down. Not right for the paper stock. Don't stick right."

"I have seen it before," said Rudy gravely. "The bill stands up to handling for a while, but in time some sort of chemical breakdown takes place."

Raider turned the bill over. "Back work is kinda messy."

"It's a disaster!" exploded the man.

"Boys," said Tunstall, "let me introduce Mr. Duncan Otis Fish III, president of the Cattleman's Bank. These fellows are Pinkertons, D.O."

Duncan Otis Fish III waved away the introduction. He looked at Raider as if any moment he would jump out of his skin.

"How did you come by this?" Tunstall asked.

"Would you believe the federal government? A whole shipment—twenty thousand in tens. Shipped down from Denver not more than a week ago."

"Whatta you talkin' about?" snapped Raider. "They don't ship paper money from the Denver mint."

"They just started last month."

"Twenty thousand!" Tunstall whistled.

"They're all over town, all over the county. Well, what the devil are you going to do, Mason?"

"Hey, hey, hey, give us a chance. These boys are on top of it. They'll track down the source."

"Pinkertons? Hah! You know something, the government is thinking of putting all counterfeiting cases into the hands of the Secret Service. Make 'em their hot potatoes exclusively."

"I wish they would," murmured Raider. "I sure don't have any great yen to go out chasin' after friggin' paper-hangers."

"Well," snarled Fish, "you're going to have to go out chasing after this bozo. Somebody has to."

"I do not understand how such a large sum could flood the town so quickly," said Rudy, "unless it is flowing directly from your bank."

"Course it is! You deaf?"

"Could be one o' your employees is behind it," observed Raider.

"Nonsense! That's bald stupid. I have nine people in full-time employ. The least time anyone of them has been with us is eleven years. That'd be Charlie Hampton. He's straight as a die. Everybody is."

"Dice been known to get loaded once in a while," said Raider airily.

"You're barking up the wrong tree, brother. I told you before, I'll say it again, that twenty thousand came straight from Denver. That's where you'll find your counterfeiter, there and no place else!"

"I'm talking about distributin'," said Raider.

"Great Scott, we're all distributing it! Unaware it's counterfeit until ten minutes ago. When Charlie spotted it. Individual passing it would hardly tip his own hand, would he? Counterfeiter's down in Denver. Probably working for the mint. Or working with somebody who is. Damnation, by now he's probably packed up and moved on!"

"Simmer down, D.O.," said Tunstall. "Getting hot under the collar isn't going to solve anything."

"I don't care what you say 'bout the people workin' for you," interposed Raider. "They could be saints. They could also be plaster saints. At least one. That's all it takes to bring the scam to town and get the ball rollin'."

Rudy turned to Tunstall. "He is right. It would not do any harm to talk to them individually."

Fish was seething. He looked as if at any moment he would burst a blood vessel. Raider could have sympathized with him had he not been so obnoxious.

"Waste of precious time!" exclaimed Fish. "I say climb on your horses and get your butts down there. Collar the people in charge and push 'em to the wall. Elroy Emerson is the general manager. Buttonhole him. If whoever's responsible isn't caught, and fast, there'll be holy hell to pay. If restitution isn't made, and quick, the Cattleman's is done for. Ruined! Cheyenne is! The whole county. Maybe even the territory!"

"Oh, shut up, D.O., give these guys a chance. They're pros, they know their business."

Raider nodded. "We'll talk to your people. If we're satisfied they're squeaky clean, like you claim, we'll head on down to Denver. Just give us a chance, give us time."

"That's the one thing I can't give a blessed soul!"

"Calm down!" burst Tunstall irritably.

"You! It's not your bank going down the drain. It's not your reputation, your acceptance and stature in the community. Gimme that!" He snatched up the bill and jammed it in his pocket. "Get on it, you two. Find whoever's behind it and get me my money back!"

Out he stomped, slamming the door in his wake, straightening the calendar.

"Friendly cuss," observed Raider.

"Pretty badly shaken, " said Tunstall. "Sweet Jesus, seven years, and not a phony penny. You two show up and suddenly it's raining bogus tens."

"Curious," mused Rudy aloud. "I would have thought he would counterfeit the twenty-dollar gold certificate." He sighed. "The *Schweinhund* has been outguessing me at every turn. And continues to. How discouraging."

"Yeah," muttered Raider. "Well, let's get on over to the bank. We need that phony ten and to sit down with his people. We find just one can't look us in the eye, it might turn out we won't have to go flyin' down to Denver after all."

By the time they reached the Cattleman's Bank, accompanied by Tunstall, word had spread county wide. A large crowd was collecting in front. Fish addressed the gathering.

"You all know me, know everybody who works for me. We're not the problem. It's the mint down in Denver that supplied us the tens. They're responsible, they'll make restitution. You have my word on it. The best thing, the smartest thing you can do is to hang on to any and all bogus tens you have, put them in a safe place and when it's time to turn them in for legitimate bills or certificates, come straight here and we'll oblige you."

"When's that gonna be, D.O.?" bawled a voice.

"Hopefully within a week's time or less."

"Hopefully?" shrilled a woman. "What's that mean?"

"Please listen. We've been caught unawares. It's been as big a shock to us as to any of you. We will make good, but we can't do so on your word. You have to have the counterfeits in hand."

"We got 'em!" shouted another man, holding up three.

Others followed his example.

"All right, all right, all right. Form a single line and the tellers will take what you have and give you an equivalent amount in other denominations."

"Fake or real?" yelled a man.

The crowd laughed. Fish scowled. He could see nothing funny. For the first time, Raider could sympathize with him.

"A run on the bank," he said to Tunstall. "Will it bust him, do you think?"

"I doubt it, but it's sure not going to do much for his ulcer. Maybe you should give him an hour for all the commotion to die down before you start questioning the help. It looks from here like they're going to be busier than a one-handed milker for a while."

They gave the crowd an hour and a half to thin out before approaching the bank. One look at Fish when they marched in established that the high-strung victim of Gerhard Steinbrenner's latest artistic effort had deteriorated markedly under the pressure of the run on his bank. He looked beaten to his knees, and when he spoke it was barely above a whisper, as if he no longer had the energy to deliver his words in a normal tone. All the considerable fight had deserted him; he was almost polite.

"There's an empty office in the corner. You can talk to them one by one. Save the tellers till last, if you don't mind. As you can see, they're still pretty busy."

"It may not be very much help," said Rudy gravely,

"nevertheless, I would like you to know that we are very sorry this happened to you, and we will do our level best to find the man responsible and bring him to justice."

"Find him with my money on him, that's all I ask."

They interviewed all nine employees, deferring to Fish's request and saving the tellers till last. Charlie Hampton was about fifty, neither ugly nor handsome, more nondescript than anything else. His was a face that, seen in a crowd, was immediately forgotten. He was a bachelor, lived by himself, no relatives in the area, no close friends. It was easy to see why he was a loner; apart from all his other social shortcomings, he had neither personality nor sense of humor. When Raider inadvertently said something funny, Rudy would smile, even laugh out loud. Charlie, however, either didn't get it or couldn't. The man was a walking cipher. He was the last employee they talked to.

"How did you discover the bill was phony?" Raider asked. "Do you remember?"

"Yes."

"You want to tell us?" Rudy asked.

"Well, it was a slow time; nobody at my window. I just, for want of something to do, picked up a ten off the top of the pile in my drawer. For some reason I looked at the back. I looked and my eyes nearly jumped out of my head."

"Messy work," said Raider.

"Really messy. The word 'silver' across the back in big sharp cut letters against a dark background. They're shaded to give them depth. Here, let me show you." He got out a ten. "You can see the shading is irregular; it comes too far down on the 'r' and not far enough on the 'i.' And look at the word 'certificate' at the bottom. It's muddy; you have to hold it no more than two inches from your eyes to read it. Further than that and they muddy up. That shouldn't be. The words 'ten dollars' on the right side, bowing around the background of the 'r' . . ."

"Muddy too," said Rudy.

Charlie turned the bill over. "The front is beautiful; the detail, the proportions, the positioning, everything. All except for the ink. I wonder why he used such cheap ink?"

"Could be that was the one thing he couldn't get his hands on when he come here," said Raider. "And had to substitute what he could get."

"I think the work was already completed before he landed," said Rudy. "He simply could not obtain the ink in Europe."

"And had to make do with what he could get."

"Right."

"We'll hang on to this, if you don't mind," said Raider, holding up the bill. "We'll tell Mr. Fish so you won't be out ten bucks."

"That's okay, I already switched some of our old genuine tens for the news ones I had. I won't be out a red cent."

They thanked him and stopped off to see Fish on the way out to thank him as well. Rudy repeated his promise to collar the counterfeiter with all due dispatch. Raider wished he wouldn't be so lavish and emphatic with his promises, but refrained from commenting.

Outside the bank Rudy paused. "Can we ride our horses down to Denver? I would like to."

"We could, but seeing we're in a rush, it's better we take the train. It's a hundred and five miles. We can be there before sundown and with any luck catch the boys at the mint before they quit for the day. We can bring the horses along in the horse car. Cost us a couple o' bucks, maybe, but I'm thinkin' we may have to trace the shipment back to here, in which case it might mean checkin' at every stop."

"How many are there?"

"There's Carr, Pierce, Greeley, Plattville, Lupton. No more'n five or six. Let's go get the horses. And cross your fingers this won't turn out a wild goose chase."

"Not one of those people struck me as suspicious. None of them acted guilty."

"Mmmmm. That still don't mean this won't turn out a wild goose chase. We'll just have to take it as it comes and hope for the best."

CHAPTER FIVE

Clark, Gruber & Company's private mint was originally erected to turn the gold dust of central Colorado's mining camps into coins proudly stamped "Pikes Peak Gold." In the wake of the great 1859 gold rush, miners and merchants alike had discovered that "dust" had certain drawbacks as a medium of exchange. Most miners carried a pocket scale to measure out the price of everything from booze to baby buggies. Even so, disputes frequently arose, with each party to a transaction suspecting the other of cheating on quality or weight.

The problem eased to an extent with the arrival of the first bankers, who bought gold dust in exchange for hard currency, then shipped the dust back east for minting. But this was expensive and time-consuming. Shippers levied a five percent express charge each way, plus another five percent for insurance coming and going. The gold had to travel by stagecoach, and it might be in transit for as long as three months.

No law existed forbidding a bank from coining its own money. The two bankers purchased coining equipment in

Philadelphia, which reached Denver by ox-team four months later.

Their first coins, minted from gold dust that contained a natural silver alloy, were worth more than the government's. When this mintage proved too soft, the firm added alloy to the dust and still turned out a product purer than federal money.

After Colorado's formal recognition as a United States territory in 1861, officials grew nervous about the propriety of a mint in their midst. In 1863, Clark, Gruber & Company's property was purchased by the federal government.

Raider and Rudy got their horses off the train, mounted up, and rode to the center of town and the Clark, Gruber brick building. The ground floor front was recessed, the second story supported by four white columns. Five steps mounted to a rear door down at the end of the right side of the building. There were three upstairs windows on all four sides. The vault was located in the basement.

The firm's name no longer graced the front of the building; the simple statement "U.S. Mint—Denver Branch" had replaced it. They arrived just in time. The workers were leaving for the day. Elroy Emerson, the man in charge, was in his office getting ready to leave. They introduced themselves. Raider showed his I.D. and explained their mission. Emerson, a slight-looking man in his fifties, clean-shaven, with a healthy crop of curly chestnut hair, exploded.

"D.O. Fish told you we shipped him counterfeit money. He's out of his mind! I check every shipment that goes out of here personally. That money was clean as a hound's tooth; genuine currency of the realm, yessiree. Come with me, you can see for yourselves. Damn him and his suspicious hide!"

He took them downstairs to the vault. A king's ransom was stacked inside.

"Those two shelves are ten-dollar silver certificates. Examine every last one if you like, you won't find a single phony."

Raider handed him Charlie Hampton's bogus bill.

"Shoddiest-looking back work I've ever seen. Obverse is top notch, though. You telling me Fish got twenty thousand dollars worth of this?"

"Somebody pulled a switch."

"Not at this end. Go ahead, examine those bills. Take your time, I got all night. This is serious business."

"We'll take your word for it," said Rudy. "Can we see the press room?"

"Ain't no such animal. We don't print. Printing's done in Philadelphia; currency's shipped here. We distribute. Only money made here is gold coins. You want to see the stamping machines?"

"We don't care about coins," said Raider.

"Would you kindly tell us the procedure from the time you receive an order to when it leaves here?" Rudy asked.

"First thing we do is check back with the bank and get a wire of confirmation. To make sure somebody at the other end doesn't phony up an order. Believe me, it's been tried. We wait until the bonds or silver or gold or old currency arrives, whatever is used in payment, full payment, then fill the order. The money is counted six times by six different individuals. It's packed in special waterproof boxes like this one here. You can see the stencil: 'Property of U.S. Army.' We can't very well stamp it 'U.S. Mint.' Two of our people escort it to the train station and guard it en route to its destination. The box is never opened for any reason until it arrives; one or the other or both men keep an eye on it every step of the way. When they arrive at their destination, they escort it to the bank and into the president's office. He opens it, double-checks the amount, and signs the delivery order in the presence of the escort. There's no way in heaven or hell that twenty thousand could be slickered out from under their noses and counterfeit money substituted."

"It appears to have happened," said Rudy.

"Impossible. If a switch was made—"

"If?" asked Raider.

"When then, damn it. It had to be at the Cheyenne

bank. After delivery. Right under Fish's nose, most likely. I've known the sonovabitch for ages; he's more interested in how he dresses and what kind of toilet water he douses himself with than business. Oh hell, not that he's careless; he's not. But the point is we delivered the goods. Intact. Twenty thousand in new tens from Philadelphia to here to Cheyenne. If you want to talk to the boys who escorted it they'll be in first thing in the morning."

"They live in town?" Raider asked.

"Sure."

"Give us their addresses and we can call on 'em tonight. That way we won't have to bother 'em on the job tomorrow. Take 'em away from their work, you know."

"Suits me. Let's go back upstairs to the office. I can look up where they live. Their names are Ed Slocum and Harley Lauricella. Been with me since the government took over here. Nineteen years come November. I trust 'em with my life. Trust everybody who works here. Let me tell you birds something—people who work for the U.S. Mint have to be on their toes, have to be as honest as the day is long. Why? On account if and when something goes wrong, they're the first to be suspected. Oh, not that bad apples haven't surfaced in the barrels once in a blue moon, but brother, it is rare. I've never had one here. You got a problem with counterfeit money? Your problem's back in Cheyenne; bet the farm on it. Not D. O. Fish; somebody working for him. He or she's the culprit.

CHAPTER SIX

The dark-haired, rangy man had the drawn and weary look about him of one who had just come out of prison or a hospital. He carried an old carpetbag, and so low was his energy level, he walked as if it were packed with bricks. He could not walk more than twenty steps without pausing to catch his breath. After his train had pulled into Union Station, he had made his way through the milling crowd to the sidewalk, coming out to the sight of a line of hansom cabs drawn up to the curb, waiting for fares. A wedge of geese plowed the sky overhead, moving southward and arguing volubly. The bright sun caused him to wince as he emerged from the shadows. He walked slowly to the second cab in the line, the first one being commandeered by two sprinting, somberly attired drummers lugging their sample cases.

"One hundred ninety-three, one hundred ninety-five Fifth Avenue, please," said the pale young man.

Twenty minutes later the horse clopped to a stop in front of a four-story building boasting a large sign affixed to the bricks between two third-floor windows: PINKERTON NATIONAL DETECTIVE AGENCY. Under it was a somewhat gro-

43

tesque-looking representation of a human eye enclosed by the legend: "The eye that never sleeps." The man paid his fare, mounted the steps, and entered the elevator. The elevator man took him to the third floor. He came out to discover the door open to the small room opposite, an undersized squirrel's nest crammed from floor to ceiling with filing cabinets. In their midst sat Emmaline Cathcart, the young lady in charge of the records room. She sat typing away vigorously.

The newcomer set his bag down and doffed his derby, holding it against his chest. "Mr. Allan Pinkerton, please."

"Mr. Pinkerton's not in at the moment." The man's face fell so suddenly and so dramatically that Emmaline felt obliged to explain, "But he'll be back. He's gone to lunch with the mayor and some other gentlemen. Mr. Wagner is in."

"Who?"

"The superintendent."

"Ahhh."

Disappointment fled, and the friendly, winning expression returned to his face.

Emmaline rose from her posture chair. "He's just down the hall."

She led the way, turning to the visitor just before they reached the fourth door on their left. "Who shall I say is calling?"

They had arrived at the door. It was wide open. The office was empty. A battered rock maple bench stood just outside.

"He's probably in another office. I'll try and find him for you."

"Thank you."

William Wagner came back before Emmaline Cathcart could find him. He paused before going into his office to stare at the stranger, his carpetbag slumping by his left leg and his hat on his lap. The man stood up, clicked his heels smartly, and bowed.

"You looking for me?"

"Mr. Pinkerton is out."

"I'm Wagner. Can I help you?"

"Rudolph Fenstermacher from Berlin, Germany."

Wagner nodded, then started as the name registered. His jaw dropped as if it were suddenly filled with birdshot.

"You're—"

"Rudolph Fenstermacher, *geheime Polizist.*"

"Come in, come in. Close the door. Sit, sit, let me have your hat." Wagner sat behind his desk, clearing the decks with his forearms. "What the hell is this?"

"I beg your pardon."

"You're Fenstermacher? You got any identification?"

"None. If you will permit me to explain."

"First, let me. Better brace yourself. This may come as a shock. A man came here last week calling himself—"

"Rudolph Fenstermacher. It does not surprise me. Tall, blond-haired, good-looking, with Bismarck mustachios?" He pantomimed their shape and dimensions on his own naked upper lip and cheeks. "Permit me to explain."

"Please do."

"The man I have just described to you is unquestionably Gerhard Steinbrenner. I have been pursuing him for three years. For three years he has eluded me. My superiors learned of his intention to leave England, where I tracked him to, for the United States. I missed his ship from Southampton by less than fifteen minutes, but was able to board a freighter. Upon arriving in New York, I set out immediately for the Pinkerton office to make contact and inform your people that Steinbrenner had arrived. How far ahead of me he was it was difficult to say, perhaps two hours, perhaps two days. At any rate, it was quite late in the afternoon. I was walking down Broadway, passing a dark alley, when I was suddenly struck on the head. It felt as if my skull had been crushed. I saw no one.

"I awoke in a hospital bed. Try as I was able, I could not remember what had happened. It was all a blank. For the first week I did not even know my own name."

"Amnesia."

"Whoever hit me evidently dragged me into the alley out of sight of passing pedestrians, robbed me, and left me for dead. I was very close to death, believe me. He took my weapon, wallet, money, identification papers, passport, everything. Even my decorations from the Franco-Prussian War."

"Steinbrenner."

"Yes. Among my effects was your chief's letter to Hauptmann Huberman, my superior. Among other things in the letter were directions on how to get from New York to here."

"So he simply stepped into your shoes and began to pose as you. He showed up here, told us his story, and we sent him west with one of our top operatives."

"To Cheyenne."

"Yes. Oh dear."

"Whoever he is teamed up with is in great danger. Steinbrenner is a master forger and counterfeiter, and as ruthless as they come: he is cunning, he is brilliant, and he will not hesitate to kill anyone who poses a threat to him."

"We'll warn Raider at once. Wait here, I'll only be a moment. Oh dear."

"What?"

"Wait till the chief hears this. He'll go through the ceiling. I'll be right back. Can I get you anything? Would you like a cigar?"

"No thank you."

Wagner rushed out and down the hall to Emmaline Cathcart's cubicle. He dictated a telegram. She took it upstairs to the telegraph room. Three minutes later Wagner returned to the office. No sooner had he sat back down than a knock sounded. It was Allan Pinkerton returned from lunch. Wagner held his breath as he introduced Rudolph Fenstermacher. Pinkerton did not explode; he reacted more stunned than angry. Indeed, the expression on the chief's face mirrored the one Wagner had felt on his own when Rudolph identified himself. Wagner hurriedly filled the chief in on the conversation up to that point.

"Raider's got to be warned, Will!"

"It's already in the works."

"Ye say that ye were hospitalized in New York following the attack?"

"For seven weeks."

"Guid losh! That'd give the nasty beggar ample time to run out to Cheyenne and set up shop."

"It would," said Wagner.

"Then come back here and launch his masquerade. The devious scoundrel! What better protection can he have than to pair up with the man who's out looking for him and pretend to be doing the same. It's absolutely ingenious! With Raider none the wiser, the scalawag can lead him about like an ox with a ring through its nose.

"As I recall in our discussions here he was somewhat vague as to how he operates. Can you tell us?"

"He has a ladyfriend, Fräulein Hauser. They have worked together for years. She is a former actress, and I am told, although I have never actually seen her, that she is extraordinarily beautiful. Steinbrenner prints a supply of counterfeit money, hands it over to her, and she sees to the distributing. Which is the most masterfully conceived phase of the entire operation."

"How is that?" Wagner asked.

"As you gentlemen are aware, counterfeit bills are usually passed by a number of people, *nicht wahr*? Steinbrenner disdains such a tactic in favor of a far simpler method. Hauser takes the money to the target city or town, registers at a local hotel, and visits all the banks. She studies the tellers at their work. She selects one, just one, and concentrates on him. And she has a positive genius for choosing the perfect individual to suit her needs."

"An excellent judge of character, eh?"

"An uncanny judge. Bank tellers are pretty much the same the world over. Every one underpaid and overworked. And under the supervision of an older man who is paid ten times their salary. If I were to describe the typical teller, a man not a woman, he would be approaching middle age, a long time stuck in the rut of the same tedious job, underpaid, as I said. Unappreciated. With little or no chance of advancement. A lone wolf, unmarried, unloved, with precious little social life. In short, a frustrated and perhaps very bitter individual. A cherry ripe for the plucking.

"Hauser fixes on him and goes to work. She cleverly stages an accidental meeting, there is a brief period devoted to getting to know each other, and within three days the poor fool falls hopelessly in love with her. How can he help it? She's beautiful, attentive, she falls all over him, sets his head spinning. By the fifth day, believe it or not, he is ready to propose marriage."

"Incredible."

"But true. At least the majority do. At that point she plays her ace. Following a bout of serious lovemaking, when he asks her to marry him, she demurs. She acts guilty; she tells him she has a confession to make. If they are to be married, she feels she owes it to him to be honest. She tells him she would love nothing better than to accept his proposal, but she cannot; she's unworthy of him because of her guilty past."

"The sneaky wench," rasped Pinkerton. "She has him in the palm of her hand."

"Exactly. He presses her to divulge her guilty secret. She puts on a great performance. She tells him she is guilty of passing counterfeit money. She's never been caught, never arrested—which is the truth—but her heart is heavy with guilt. And because she loves him she cannot bring herself to deceive him. It is at this point that her acting skills are at their best, she is most convincing."

"The poor sap is blinded by her beauty," said Wagner. "She's got him around her little finger. She could talk him into murdering his mother."

"Practically. She confesses all, begs his understanding, and he cannot forgive all fast enough. At this point she risks all and tells him she has a quantity of counterfeit money in her possession, an almost perfect replica of the real thing; German marks, French or Belgian francs, British pounds, American dollars. She shows him a specimen. It is excellent work, it always is. He is very impressed. He is also as poor as a church mouse. She herself has little money. If working together they can pass her counterfeit, exchange it for the real thing, they will be—"

"On easy street!" boomed the chief.

"By this time she can be ninety-nine percent certain that the poor fool will jump at the bait and swallow the hook," said Wagner.

"Correct. If he does hesitate, she points out how poor they are, how easy it will be. She sells him on the idea. She suggests they line up a number of people as passers. Which affords him the chance to make his first contribution: he suggests the obvious. Why bring in outsiders? Why not entrust him with the entire amount and, when he gets the chance, when the danger of discovery is practically nil, he will exchange it for an equivalent amount of genuine currency."

"She congratulates him on his brilliant idea," said Wagner.

The chief nodded. "He does it, and what happens next?"

"He brings it back to the hotel to her after work that day. They make their plans for the future. To prevent any possibility of suspicion, in case the switch should be discovered —it never is so soon—he returns to work the next day. The bogus money is so good it is not discovered sometimes for weeks, so he is in no danger. That night, when the bank closes, he hurries back to the hotel to be reunited with his love."

"To find the bird has flown," said Wagner.

"Leaving him with empty pockets, a ruptured conscience, the fear of God in his heart, and Lord knows what else."

"It is a strategy Hauser and Steinbrenner have worked over and over; it has yet to fail. I am sure they will try it again in Cheyenne."

"They nae doubt already have!" boomed the chief. "They've had more than enou' time. Poor Raider, running around with the devil himself and suspecting nae a thing."

Rudy suddenly appeared on the verge of collapse. He complained of a headache.

"You look ill, my boy," said Pinkerton solicitously. "Come with me to my office and lie down."

Pinkerton nodded to Wagner, took Rudy next door into his office, and settled him on his new Sears, Roebuck fringed Turkish couch.

"I'm afraid I have been overdoing it," said Rudy. "Trying to make up for lost time."

"Relax, go to sleep, why dinna you."

He summoned his first-shift secretary, Martha-Mary Albertson, from her adjacent office to find a blanket to put over Rudy. He then went back to Wagner's office.

"What now?" Wagner asked.

"We must double-check. Get a cablegram off to Berlin asking for his physical description. The two are so markedly different in appearance it should be all we need to identify the real Rudy."

"You don't think this fellow's a fake?"

"I dinna know what to think. I only know we've already been burnt once; we'd be foolish to take anything for granted or any stranger's word from here on in."

"And what if he does check out, as I'm sure he will. What's our next move?"

"We'll both have to think about that. We'll probably end up sending him out with one of our people to try and track down Raider and Steinbrenner."

"He's in no condition to travel, not right away. Looks to me like the trip out here practically killed him."

"We'll give him a day or two to rest up. One thing is to our advantage, Will. Steinbrenner has nae idea he's been discovered. The last he knew he left Rudy for dead in that alley in New York."

"True, but I fail to see how that helps Raider."

"Raider's a big boy; he knows how to protect himself."

"He just doesn't know when, not if he doesn't suspect Steinbrenner. I sure wouldn't want to be in his shoes."

"Foosh! There you go, imagining the worst." He got up and went to his own office door. "Martha-Mary." She joined him in the hall. He closed the door.

"He's asleep, Chief."

"Go upstairs to the telegraph room. Tell Walter to arrange for a cablegram to be sent to the Berlin police. You have the address in your file. We need an accurate description of *geheime Polizist* Rudolph Fenstermacher as soon as possible. Get right on it, please."

"Yes, sir."

Rudolph Fenstermach dozed away the rest of the afternoon. Pinkerton let him sleep, carrying on business as usual around his prostrate form. At three o'clock the chief's second-shift secretary, Anna Frankenthaler, relieved Martha-Mary Albertson. At six-thirty that evening, after the office closed, and the chief, Anna, and Walter Cody, the chief telegrapher, were among the few who continued working, Pinkerton went upstairs. The message to Berlin had been sent to the local Western Union office and there relayed to New York and underseas via cable to Southampton and thence to the Continent and Berlin. As the chief walked in, the response arrived. The description tallied with that of the dozing Rudy to a tee.

CHAPTER SEVEN

Raider and Rudy questioned the two guards who had escorted the shipment to the Cattleman's Bank. They spoke to them at great length and separately. Each expressed amazement when told that the $20,000 in tens had turned up counterfeit. Both strenuously denied any dereliction of duty on their part. Both insisted, as Elroy Emerson had, that when they brought the box into D. O. Fish's office it was unopened and not out of their sight for so much as two seconds all the way from the mint vault. Rudy was satisfied. Raider was skeptical but stumped.

They stood outside Ed Slocum's house discussing the situation. The sky was strewn with stars, the full moon eyed them stonily, a soft but chilling breeze curled down from the heights of the Front Range of the Rockies, and Raider spat irritably.

"Wild goose chase, just like I tolja."

"We had to come down."

"Now we gotta go back."

"By train."

"By horse. You heard Lauricella. There's Irondale, Henderson, Brighton, Lupton, Platteville, Greeley, Eaton,

Pierce, an' Carr. Nine stops. Nine chances to pull a switch. We gotta stop at each depot an' double-check; see if they're tellin' the truth."

"Their stories were identical."

"So what? They could easily have put their heads together an' agreed on one. They sure had plenty o' time. We gotta check with every station master, every ticket seller on the way. We describe Slocum and Lauricella to 'em and see if either one or both is recognized as gettin' off or on durin' the stop."

"If they were smart neither one would; if they were working with a third party, that person would get on, make the switch, and get off. And if that is the case, we have no idea what *they* look like."

"Damn, you're right. Oh hell, let's stop off anyhow. It won't take us outta our way, and we won't spend more'n twenty minutes or so questionin' folks at each depot. Whatta you say? If we start out bright and early we can be back middle of the day after tomorrow."

"That is fine with me. I cannot wait to ride my horse."

"Yeah? Well you may not be so eager by the time we get there. It's over a hundred miles, not exactly a canter round the barn. Let's go get us a bottle and hit the hay. Separate rooms, o' course."

"Of course."

"The "hay" was not fated to follow the bottle in sequence. In the saloon they stopped by on the way to the Auraria House hotel, where they encountered two lovelies: a flaming redhead for Raider, a blonde even blonder than Rudy for Mr. Mustache. Pinkerton and partner went their separate ways, beginning with separate tables. Raider set the bottle of Ruckus Juice in the center of the table and blew the dust out of both their tumblers. Demonstrating his customary tact and gentility, he poured himself a drink, downed it, and poured the lady half a drink.

"Name's John O'Toole, what's yours?"

"Hedda Winkleman," she tittered. "But don't think I call myself that. Not if I want folks to take me seriously, I don't." She batted her eyes and shifted her breastworks—a hanky demurely stuffed in her décolletage—provocatively. Raider blinkèd and hurled his drink down.

"You can call me Blaze. You know, fire—for my red hair."

"Is it real?"

"Does it make any difference?"

She seemed suddenly annoyed. He had no idea why.

"It's beautiful, whatever it is."

"Thanks. What brings you to Denver, John?"

"Business. I peddle Glidden wire."

"How come you're not out making the rounds of the wheat farms?"

"On account it's after dark and most folks are gettin' ready to turn in." He stifled a pretended yawn. "It's gettin' on to my own bedtime. You tired?"

"Not really. Thirsty, though."

He glanced to the left. Rudy was on his feet and offering his arm to his lady. He threw Raider a wave as they walked out. Fast worker, thought Raider. He'd be in bed and at work and done and thank you and good night before the two of them got to the bottom of the bottle. He eyed her as she drank. She wasn't nearly as pretty as Imogene, nor as well-endowed, but at the moment she looked a helluva lot better than the dismal prospect of spending the night by his lonesome.

"How's 'bout we take the bottle with us?"

"Where?"

"Your place?"

It crossed his mind that enjoying her hospitality would save him a dollar and thereby offset the price of her services.

"I don't have a place," she answered.

"Oh."

"Do you?"

"I expect I can get one, all right. I guess we can share. The freight, that is."

"You mean the price of the room?"

"Do I look like a cheapskate to you?"

"Oh no, no . . . not at all."

"I got money, I just have to be be careful that I don't throw it around. Expenses been runnin' high lately, what with the double funeral an' all."

"Double . . ."

"My brother an' sister. They were comin' out from Detroit to visit me. Got killed in a train wreck. I buried 'em both last week in the cemetery in Greeley. They're layin' side by side. Been carryin' my grief like a boulder inside my chest since. Saddest day of my life, standin' over the grave sayin' goodbye. We were close as skin. I sure will miss ol' Roy and sweet Jenny." He wiped away a nonexistent tear.

"You poor soul . . . I'm so sorry. Is there anything I can do?"

"Sure."

"I know just how you feel. My whole family was wiped out in a flood: Daddy, Ma, Uncle Ned, Aunt Avna, my two brothers and three sisters. Remember when the Mississippi jumped its banks and flooded clear down to Cranfield in Adams County four years ago? Biggest loss of life and property in history, according to the newspapers. Took away all nine of my loved ones in one fell swoop. Grandpa was the only survivor, and he didn't last but three weeks more. Doctor said he passed away out of grief at the loss, poor soul."

"Oh, that is rotten luck."

"I still miss 'em all. Especially at supper round the table."

"I'll bet. Whatta you say we finish this bottle, go find us a bed, an' . . ."

"What?"

"See what happens."

He winked. She tittered and clasped his hand.

They lay under the sheet as naked as two just-hatched jays. With her clothes off she was some sight for sore eyes, suffering eyes, eyes in any condition still able to see. Now with the lamp out he was ready and raring to go; there was only one barrier blocking the swift ascent to Paradise. In telling him about her family tragedy, one recollection inspired the next with the result that she couldn't stop talking. From bottle to bed she hauled him by the ears back to her childhood, to Sunday-school picnics, through the sixth grade, through good cotton crops and poor, into and out of her four marriages, through sickness and through health, through poverty, destitution, on and on and on.

"I left Mississippi vowing I'd never go back. Too many sad memories. I . . ."

He didn't hear; he was fast asleep. She woke him.

"Let me tell you about my second cousin, Alberta-Sue Winger. She was a fast woman who married a preacher. Only he turned out faster than her. Between 'em . . ."

"Hey . . ."

"What?"

"If you don't wanna mess around, do me a favor: shut up and lemme sleep."

"Oh, but there's tons more."

On she rattled. He closed his ears and reflected on women in general: this redheaded talking machine, Imogene in Cheyenne, all the Imogenes jumping in and out of his life, in and out of his bed back through his years as a Pinkerton. All over the West, Mexico, southern Canada. What a useless lot they were! What a waste of space and breathable air. Far more trouble than they were worth, millstones with lipstick around a man's defenseless neck. Queens of complaint, nags and shrews, hellcats, hellhags, hussies, and harridans. Pests, scolds, and drunks. Painted cats, sluts, hookers, and hustlers; frail and tail. Chicks, tricks, bags, and beaver. By any name, trouble in high spades: headaches, heartaches, ball-busters. A man couldn't believe 'em, couldn't trust 'em, rely on 'em, confide in 'em. Their only reason for being was to build a man up so they could tear him down. Trouble, grief, disappointment, and misery; and a mouth that never stopped.

What man had ever done to deserve 'em, what crime, what sin could be so monstrous that God's punishment should be their presence, their infestation of this world, was beyond him. He loathed and despised them all, and pitied Doc for falling into Lucinda's clutches.

He turned his head to eye Blaze in the darkness, which would have been pitch black had it not been for the moonlight shafting through the window onto the bare floor, and the feeble glow emanating from it. She appeared to be dozing. He was suddenly outraged, furious with her. She was all women, their failings, their rottenness, meanness, evil. He wanted to lash out in retaliation against her heartlessness toward him. He drew his right leg upward and turned on his left side. Using one knee and both hands, he would shove her out of bed. Bust her hip, crack her skull, the tease, the cold, unfeeling, tantalizing Jezebel!

She woke. She turned and smiled. Then threw an arm around his neck and kissed him lustily. Then she eyed him. "Anytime you're ready, John O'Toole."

He awoke the next morning giddy with love. He adored her. She didn't charge him a penny. His heart beat madly and a wave of sadness surged through him when they parted on the hotel veranda. She walked away waving; he blew her a parting kiss. What a woman, he thought, what a glorious, marvelous, considerate, affectionate human being!

Five minutes later Rudy came down.

Riding back and stopping at every town the Denver to Cheyenne run stopped at to question station employees proved a waste of time. Disappointed and frustrated, Raider bought a bottle of dollar rye in Brighton and from there on tugged on it regularly. In the middle of the afternoon they left Platteville en route to LaSalle, a stop Raider hadn't figured on when he listed the stations off the top of his head earlier. He reckoned the distance between the two towns to be about twelve miles. They were halfway to LaSalle when Rudy's horse stepped into a shallow hole and faltered. They got down and examined its right foreleg. Raider then walked off ten paces.

"Bring her over at a trot."

The horse did not hang her head to one side, did not limp, but neither was absolute proof that she hadn't injured herself. Raider again examined her leg below the knee.

"The level of the poll isn't rising and falling with each step. That's a good sign."

"You think she is injured?"

"I think we should give her ten minutes or so. If she's hurting her leg'll stiffen up. If it doesn't, she's okay."

They had been traveling through sugar beet and livestock farm country with the Front Range looming high to their left and the tracks a quarter mile to the right. They had stopped by a large, irregular outcropping. Suddenly three figures rose above the rock.

"Oh boy," mumbled Raider.

Arapahos—young, strong, tough-looking warriors. This was Arapaho country, and that of the northern Cheyenne, their longtime allies against the Crow or Sioux or any other tribe that ventured into their hunting grounds. They wore buckskins embellished with beadwork and porcupine quill bibs to protect their chests. One, much taller than the others, as tall as a Cheyenne, affected a tall, black bowler, with a single hawk feather thrust into the brim. With the black dome adding to his height, he looked seven feet tall. All three wore scalps at their belts, and two carried nine-foot lances. Bowler Hat carried an ancient, rusty, .44-caliber, 16-shot Henry, no doubt lifted from some unfortunate trapper when his scalp was lifted. They also wore rattlesnake-skin-covered horn bows over their shoulders and otter-skin quivers filled with arrows. They were tipsy; not roaring drunk and falling off their ponies, just feeling good and brazen enough to make a fuss.

"Red Indians," said Rudy matter-of-factly.

"Drunk enough to make trouble."

Rudy drew his Gruener.

"Put that away, Chrissakes! There could be a hundred more outta sight back there with these three clowns ridin' point for 'em."

Rudy restored his pistol to his shoulder holster.

"You fire that thing, we'll both wind up with our hair on their belts. I'll handle this."

Bowler Hat dismounted and came forward, strutting arrogantly, leading his scrawny pony. "Whiskey!"

Raider sighed. Rudy studied all three, his expression pure fascination. Raider got the bottle out of his saddlebag and held it out.

"Brave Arapaho warriors, *cheena-he-da*, whiskey."

Bowler Hat snatched it rudely as his companions dismounted. He downed nearly a quarter of the remaining contents. Rudy gasped in astonishment. Barely two inches remained in the bottle when Bowler Hat lowered it. He studied it, frowning. One of the others stepped forward and snatched it from him. He drank. The third finished the bottle.

"Whiskey all gone," muttered Bowler Hat.

"No kiddin'," growled Raider.

"More whiskey."

"Got no more."

One of the others went to his saddlebags and dug through them, throwing the contents on the ground.

"No more, I told ya!"

"No more whiskey, you give guns and belts to us. Then you ride away."

"Oh say, friend, *amigo,* blood brother, you don't want us to do that. You wouldn't leave us defenseless against varmits and critters and snakes; outlaws who'd rob us blind if we couldn't defend ourselves. Out here in the wilds. You might as well steal our clothes and boots as to take our hardware, leave us naked and unarmed."

Bowler Hat cocked the Henry, raised, it, and pushed the muzzle up to within ten inches of Raider's face.

"Guns and belts."

"Oh for Chri . . . Okay, okay, have it your friggin' way. Give him your popgun, Rudy. Lift it out easy, friendly-like, thumb an' forefinger on the grip only. Easy an' slow an'—"

It was as far as he got. Rudy whipped out his Gruener and blasted Bowler Hat squarely in the heart. His hat jumped from his head, his eyes jumped from their sockets, his chest blossomed. He sank to his knees and dropped on his face. Before Raider could move a muscle, before either of the others could react, before the first smoke could escape the muzzle of Rudy's gun, arrows came flying at them, whirring ominously, singing their death song. Raider and Rudy threw themselves flat. One of the redskins did likewise; the other was a split second too slow. Two arrows thudded into this chest, killing him

Raider crabbed toward the protection of the rock, his teeth clenched, heart pounding, expecting an arrow to plow into him in the next second. The attackers began whooping; he could hear galloping, hooves stomping the earth beneath this chest. Rudy scrambled up beside him. The surviving Arapaho joined them. Rudy started up for a quick look. Raider grabbed him, pullling him down.

Just in time. A flurry of arrows zipped through the space his head had vacated. The sound of additional riders reached their ears. It came from the opposite direction. Raider gestured, indicating a cut in the rock to their left ten or twelve feet away. They slithered toward it. He was the first to reach it, dropping into it, turning his body as he fell. Rudy came down on top of him. The Indian fell on Rudy; their combined weight crushed Raider.

"Hey! Chrissakes, whatta ya tryin' to do!"

He squirmed out from under, bringing his head up to the sight of an arrow plunging a third of they way up its shaft into the Arapaho's back. Raider sighed and pulled his body off Rudy.

"What do we do?" Rudy asked breathlessly.

"Get up an' dance. Whatta you think? Stay put, still as two stumps, eyes closed, play dead."

"But they will see us and cut our hair off."

"Shut up, lemme think. First, let's have a look. You keep down."

He shot upward, looked one way then the other, and dropped.

"Arapahos and Crows. Gotta be Crows; they're about the only Plains Injuns wear their hair long and loose, no braid. What in hell they're doin' this far south beats me. Likely chasin' somethin' or somebody. Must be fifty, and just as many Arapahos. Goin' at it hammer and tongs, like to wipe each other out. And here we sit smack in the middle in the two-buck seats!"

"What about our horses?"

"You think they're worryin' about us? Forget 'em. Just keep your head down and your tail. Hey, I got an idea. You get down the bottom like flat. I'll get on top o' you an' pull his corpse down on top o' me."

"You will crush every bone in my body! You get on the bottom."

"Forget it."

The yelling and whooping was coming uncomfortably close.

"It really is bloodcurdling," rasped Rudy worriedly.

Raider could hear the battle and see it in his eyes. Thinking as he assessed the intensity of his fear that the German could see his own in his just as clearly. The fighting sounded as if it was moving toward its height. Arrows and lances whirled over their heads in profusion. An occasional rifle cracked. The combatants screamed, fell from their ponies, and died in the dust. Ponies whinnied and toppled, tumbling riders from their backs.

The war cries rose in pitch. Raider watched Rudy suppress a shudder, though not completely. A Crow came scrambling up onto the ledge, bringing his painted face and wild eyes to within six feet of Raider's. Knife in hand, he rose to attack. There was a loud thump. Down he fell, cracking his skull on the rock, a spontoon tomahawk deep in his back.

"*Lieber Gott*," murmured Rudy, staring transfixed at the sightless eyes and the death wound.

"Stay down! How many times I got to tell you!"

Was the Crow the first and last to come upon the ledge after them? If another came or an Arapaho they certainly couldn't shoot him. That would only bring others. He reholstered his gun. They waited and listened. Raider noted

Rudy's lips moving. Was he praying? he wondered. After what seemed eons, agonizingly slow-to-arrive silence descended upon the area. The last war cry died as distance drew it from their hearing. The last hoofbeat faded.

Rudy started up. Raider snarled and grabbed his arm.

"Wait. Not yet."

He cocked an ear. He could hear murmuring. Someone laughed. Absolute silence, then activity: feet scrambling, the soft swish of a knife, low talking.

"They're takin' trophies." whispered Raider. "They'll be done and outta here in a few minutes. Just keep down."

"I'm getting stiff."

"I don't care if you cramp all the way up to your eyeballs, don't move! And don't talk. They got ears sharp as a gopher's."

The lingering survivors completed their grisly task, mounted up, and withdrew. Still Raider and Rudy did not move. Then, after fully ten more minutes, Raider got slowly to his feet.

"All clear."

Rudy came up by his side. Bloody corpses littered the battlefield. Raider counted more than forty, and an equal number of ponies. Nine-foot war lances were jammed into the ground; arrows were everywhere, strewn as far as the eye could see.

"Friggin' massacre," growled Raider.

"I wonder who won?" Rudy asked.

"I don't. I don't care. Let's cross our fingers our horses didn't get killed, wander off, or get stolen."

They found both horses. Rudy's was dead; Raider's, with an arrow in its flank and another protruding from its throat, was dying. He shot it through the head. It kicked and lay still.

"Let's get outta here before the circlin' birds come down."

He looked overhead. Five buzzards rode a thermal draft effortlessly. Two more were coming to join them. Raider retrieved his empty saddlebags, slinging them over his shoulder.

"You finally got to see your red Injun after all. Let's go, it's about six miles to LaSalle. We can catch a train from there back to Cheyenne."

CHAPTER EIGHT

Raider was footsore, weary, and at his grouchiest by the time they reached LaSalle. He refused to question anyone at the depot about Slocum and Lauricella. While Rudy did, he bought himself another bottle and resumed his tippling.

By the time they got to Cheyenne he was decently drunk and so exhausted Rudy had to help him down the steps and onto the platform. It was only 9:20 by the station clock.

"I'm goin' back an' turnin' in."

"Are you not going to have supper? I am famished."

"Frig it. I got ten little men inshide my head with shledgesh tryin' to bust out. Mere shight o' food an' I'll air my paunsch all over the friggin' table. She you in the mornin'. If I'm shtill alive."

"You drank much too much."

"Yeah."

Rudy walked him across the lobby to the stairs. Before they reached them the night clerk called to Raider.

"Telegram came in for you, Mr. O'Toole."

"Give it here."

65

"Not here, down at Western Union."

"Oh for Chrishakes. Do me favor, Rudy, sh . . . sh . . . shtop off an' pickitub."

"Of course."

"Read it. Don't bring it back. I can wait on it till . . . till."

"Shall I help you up to your room?"

"Naw. If I fall down, I can crawl resht o' the way. G'night."

Rudy ran out of the hotel and hurried down the street to Western Union. The man behind the counter pulled the door shade down in his face.

"We're closed. Open tomorrow eight o'clock sharp."

"Open the door!"

Back up went the shade. In the four seconds it had been down fear replaced the indifferent expression on the face behind the glass. The man unlocked the door. "Listen brother . . ."

"You have a telegram for Mr. O'Toole. Let me have it, I am in a hurry."

"You him?"

"Of course."

He went behind his counter, flipped through his daily file, and handed him the envelope. In his haste to get at the message, he ripped it nearly in half.

> BEWARE BEWARE BEWARE STOP MAN WORKING
> WITH YOU NOT RF BUT HIS QUARRY GS STOP S
> ARMED DANGEROUS WILL NOT HESITATE KILL
> YOU IF NECESSARY STOP BE ON GUARD ALL
> TIMES STOP AT FIRST SAFE OPPORTUNITY OVER-
> COME AND REMAND CUSTODY LOCAL LAW STOP
> RF ARRIVED HERE FROM NY TODAY STOP RE-
> COVERED FROM NEAR DEATH AT HANDS S STOP
> ADDITIONAL INFO TO FOLLOW STOP REPEAT RE-
> PEAT BE ON GUARD BEWARE
> WW

"A warning. Am I glad I got it in time. How can I ever thank you?"

"I got to close up now."

"Please, can you send a message for me?"

"Not tonight. I got to close up. Company rule: No orders taken, no messages sent after nine-thirty or before eight A.M. If the president himself walked in here . . ."

"I would be willing to pay handsomely."

"Oh? How handsome would that be?"

"Ten dollars."

"Ten!"

He was suddenly galvanized to action. He dropped his somewhat overbearing "you're-at-my-mercy" attitude and became almost servile. He snatched up a pencil and brought out a pad.

"What'll it be, sir?"

"Ah, let me see. 'Message received.' No, no, strike that. I have it: 'Reliable information acquired here today stop your man accurately described reported active Provo, Utah, stop. Get there fastest way possible.' Sign it W W."

"Got it. Don't understand it, but I got it."

"Type it out on your machine on the tape, put it on a form and in an envelope."

"Brother, for ten bucks I'll wrap it in gold leaf!"

"And oh yes, indicate that it came from the same place as this one."

"Chicago? How come?"

"Ten dollars."

"Right, right."

"And five more if you forget about it completely the moment I am out the door."

"What telegram you talking about?"

"Excellent."

Moments later he handed Rudy the envelope with a theatrical flourish and Rudy handed him a five-dollar bill and a ten. The man studied the ten.

"This isn't one of those phonies that have been coming out of the Cattleman's Bank lately, is it?"

"Definitely not. It is absolutely genuine. I understand that those bills smeared at the corners if you rub them hard enough. Try rubbing that one."

He did so; it didn't smear.

"Some mess the bank's got itself into. Thank the Lord my account's at the Farmers and Merchants. You hear the latest?"

"What is that?"

"Charlie Hampton. He's one o' Fish's tellers. Blew his brains out last night."

"Is that a fact?"

"Found him in his room. All sorts of rumors flying around. Folks are saying he not only passed out the phonies, he printed 'em up, too. Poor Charlie, I guess he just couldn't take all the tongues waggling. Either that or he figured he was a goner and would wind up in the penitentiary over in Rawlins. Anything else I can do for you? I got all night. At your service."

"That is all, thank you. Good night."

He walked back the way he came, patting the yellow envelope in his pocket and congratulating himself on his enviable presence of mind. Then his thoughts drifted back to that afternoon. He prided himself on his many assets of character and was particularly pleased with his nerve and coolness under pressure, but the encounter with the Arapahos and Crows still had him on edge. He felt a twinge of envy, thinking about the real Rudy Fenstermacher and the detective's medals pinned to his undershirt. He rather wished they were rightfully his. Fenstermacher had distinguished himself in the war under fire. But had he ever been threatened with death from all sides simultaneously, as he and Raider had been that afternoon? He had to hand it to Raider—he certainly knew how to conduct himself in a dangerous situation.

His stomach rumbled. He was so hungry he could eat a steak dinner and down a second one for dessert. He passed a restaurant, not even slowing his step to deliberate whether or not to go in. There was one more thing that needed attending to before he could relax over dinner and a bottle of wine. He quickened his step, crossed the street, and approached the door to his rented house. Instead of getting out his key, he knocked. The door opened at once.

She was indeed "extraordinarily beautiful," her hair dark as a raven's wing and shining, her mouth full, sensuous, and inviting, her beauty classic, the pattern of her features perfect. She wore a somewhat severe-looking, high lace-collared black dress that gave her the look of a spinster schoolmarm, but when she threw her slender arms around his neck, pulled him over the sill, and kissed him passionately, it was scarcely a display one might expect from a spinster.

"Gerhard, Liebchen."

"Brünnhilde."

He locked and bolted the door, then drew both front window shades.

"Where on earth have you been?" she asked.

He explained his absence. She had made tea. They sat at the kitchen table.

"What has happened to me since New York is unbelievable, but you first. What is this I hear, the teller has killed himself? My sweet, I hold your ability to break hearts in the highest esteem, but to drive a man to suicide . . ."

"Last night. I overheard two people discussing it in the street this morning. That was the first I learned of it. I was stunned."

"You saw him last night?"

"Briefly, and very early. Right after he got out of work. I was waiting for him at his rooming house to tell him we could not leave town together just yet."

"Why not?"

"I didn't know where you'd gone, when you'd be back . . ."

"I see, but how does that affect you and your itinerary. You're supposed to be on your way to San Francisco."

"Without my supply of counterfeit money?"

"Of course, you were right to linger. But about

Hampton, you did see him? What did you say to him? What sort of state was he in when you left him?"

"He was fine."

"Brünnhilde . . ."

"I swear. I did nothing to cause him to . . . Oh, he was impatient to leave, but when I told him we could not, not for a day or so, and he asked why, I explained that his leaving so soon after the discovery of the counterfeit tens would only cast suspicion on him. I pointed out that delaying our departure was to his advantage, the best possible protection for him. I even came up with a new twist. I urged him to go to Fish and tell him that his doctor had advised him to quit his job and move away. That he was a very sick man, and that he would have to move to a warm climate as soon as possible."

"Rather transparent."

"He swallowed it."

"Ah me, love not only blinds, it addles the brain. So he is out of the picture; no great loss to anyone, least of all us."

"He was such a weakling, such a gullible, trusting soul. So sad. He was crazy about me."

"They all are."

"Aren't you the least bit jealous?"

"Of course. Insanely. Ha ha. But to business. I want you to leave for San Francisco early tomorrow morning. First thing. Take the stage coach to Pine Bluffs."

"Pine . . . ?"

"It is directly east of here, near the Nebraska border."

"But that is the opposite direction."

"It is. Must I remind you, we cannot be too careful. It is possible, a chance in a million perhaps, that some-one—Fish, possibly, or one of his other employees—anyone could tie you up with Hampton. Even with him dead, if they are somehow able to determine that he was responsible for getting the tens into circulation and you, a stranger in town, were seen with him, if you are seen boarding the train west you could be traced all the way to the coast."

"That is nonsense. They can suspect he did it, but not prove it, and no one saw us together. We met only in his room and mine at the hotel, never going up the stairs together. And oh yes, once outside of town, the night he proposed and I accepted. That is what stuns me about his suicide. I was still here. We were to be married, he thought."

"Who knows what went through his mind. Who cares?"

"My point is there is no need to remind me to be careful this late in our little game together."

"Just do as I ask. The stagecoach to Pine Bluffs."

She got a thick stack of tens, fives, and twenties out of her handbag and gave them to him.

"It's all there except my expenses. What about my counterfeit for the next job?"

"Already printed. It, the inks, the stock I have left, everything except the press, are in a large carton stuffed up the chimney. The press is under the bed in my room."

He finished his tea. They went into the front room. He thrust his hand up the chimney and got the carton down.

"Incidentally, my expenses came to about fifty dollars," she said.

"How very frugal."

"Am I not always?"

"You are my right arm. Without you I would not be able to move a *pfennig*."

"I could do just as good a job as Frau Steinbrenner."

"Patience, my dear. When we retire."

"And when is that?"

"Perhaps as early as next year. When we are finished in North America."

"I still owe for my hotel room."

He counted out $400. "When you get to San Francisco, register at the Crocker House. Here's your expense money, and here's your counterfeit. Count it when you get a chance. There should be thirty thousand. You may begin searching out a suitable contact as soon as you arrive, but do not approach him until I get there. I will be a week, possibly longer."

"Why the delay? We're finished here. I think we should both move on."

"Brünnhilde, I must tell you, and do not think me crazy: I have never had so much fun in my life! Apart from which, there is still unfinished business."

"Fun?"

"Just listen. I got to Chicago and went straight to the Pinkertons, posing as Fenstermacher, of course. Their chief paired me up with one of his operatives to go chasing after the notorious Gerhard Steinbrenner, a chap by the name of Raider. The man is a revelation, a classic. You have never met anyone like him. There is no one. He is uncouth, uncultured, uneducated, dresses like a tramp—and he is the most amusing man I have ever met, a three-ring circus. Without meaning to be. That is one side of him; the other is fascinating. I make him sound like a stupid oaf, an *Esel, Scharfskopf,* eh? He is the furthest thing from either. In his crude way he is positively brilliant! Shrewd, incredibly resourceful, knows everything about everything out here: liquor, horses, weapons, red Indians and their ways, the territory like you know your beautiful face in the mirror."

"*Am* I beautiful, Gerhard?"

"Please, let me finish. He is cool as ice under fire, courageous, tough as they come. If necessary, I am sure he would not hesitate to battle a mountain lion barehanded."

"He sounds like something out of Till Eulenspiegel's imagination."

"He is truly larger than life: astonishing, fascinating, and I am enjoying myself immensely!"

He told her about faking the telegram and that the first thing in the morning he and Raider would be off to Provo, Utah.

"But why? You're not making sense."

"It makes excellent sense. Brace yourself. Fenstermacher has reached Chicago."

"But he's dead. You—"

"He survived. I hit him with a brick. A brick! As hard as I could. His skull has to be plate steel. He went down like a tree. I dragged him into the alley out of sight, checked to see if he was breathing; he was not. I emptied his pockets and got out of there as fast as I could."

"Too fast. You should have been more thorough."

He patted her cheek and smiled. "So he lived; it is no problem. We have eluded him for three years, and we will continue to. To be honest, I am not sorry I did not kill him. Frankly, I have come to enjoy our little cat and mouse."

"That's foolish talk. You should have killed him when you had the chance."

"My, but we are bloodthirsty."

"You should have ! Talk about me taking chances!"

"I did not! Enough. He is no threat; no more now than he was in Europe. To change the subject: As you know, before we left England I planned in advance every move we would make when we got here."

"I still do not understand why we had to come all the way out here. What is the difference between Berlin and New York, London and Boston?"

"Think about it. The police in the large eastern cities are numerous and well organized. Many of them do not wear badges in plain sight and therefore cannot be detected. Added to which, I am unfamiliar with their methods, their technical expertise. I know no counterfeiters this side of the ocean and cannot compare notes. Would not if I could. Out here the law is—how do I say it?—weakly enforced. A handful of men under a sheriff or marshal are responsible for covering vast stretches of territory, people scattered far and wide. Their resources, their methods of investigation, of detection are primitive."

"Perhaps not so primitive in San Francisco, my love."

"Ah, but now we are finished here, we have experience. We cannot help but meet with success out there. After that we will work our way back east. If, heaven forbid, there is a slip-up and we are unsuccessful on the West Coast, we

can always head south over the border. I have heard the
Mexicans are as primitive as the Americans out here. We
should do very well."

"I still don't see why you must run off to Utah."

"I already told you. Besides, as I say, Fenstermacher is
in Chicago, but sooner or later he will come out here. He
may be already on his way. Let him come. Let him arrive,
stew, and fester while Raider and I are away. In the meantime, I have the benefit of Raider's companionship. Apart
from amusing me, he is unwittingly teaching me all about
the West. When he begins to bore me, I will do away with
him."

"When you're rid of him you'll come back after Fenstermacher?"

"Why bother? He will have no way of knowing where I
have gone to. What can he do but sit and wait and wonder
and, when he runs out of patience, give it up as a bad job
and go back to Chicago. Praying that should any leads
develop they will find their way to Pinkerton headquarters,
right?"

"I still say why bother with Utah. Raider is in a drunken
stupor, he'll sleep through the night. By morning we could
be two hundred miles from here."

"And hangover and all, he would come after us. Did I
neglect to mention tenacity when I listed his attributes?
Have you eaten supper? I am starving. We musn't be
seen together. I will go out and get something to eat."

"I am hungry myself."

"Give me ten minutes, then go out the back way. I will
be dining at the Laramie Restaurant up the street across
from Western Union. You will find yourself another place
as far from there as possible. After you dine, go straight
back to your hotel and pack. You have your money and
your orders; there is no need for us to see each other again
here. Remember, when you check into the Crocker House,
do not engage the contact you pick until I get there, just in
case I might find reason in the meantime to alter our strategy."

"Business, business, business, it's all you talk about!"

She grabbed him and kissed him soulfully. He had to break it to catch his breath.

"Good night, *Liebling*. See you in San Francisco."

"Mmmmmm. I love you, Gerhard. Look, your bedroom is only ten steps away."

"Not now. One must be in the mood. I have too much on my mind."

"Business."

"I love you, Brünnhilde."

"If you did, you would marry me."

"Good night, *Liebling*."

CHAPTER NINE

In an effort to hasten Rudy Fenstermacher's recovery, Allan Pinkerton magnanimously invited him to be his and Jean's house guest. It would, he averred, be much more comfortable than a hotel, and he would be among friends. Husband and wife and guest sat at dinner on the evening of the latter's third day in Chicago. Rudy made no effort to conceal his anxiety and impatience to resume the chase. Unfortunately, his periodic headaches lingered, and he still felt weak. They were in the midst of dessert: homemade peach cobbler—Jean's favorite recipe—when Rudy apologized and asked to be excused.

"Something wrong with your peach cobbler, lad?" Pinkerton asked.

"It is delicious, only I suddenly have a headache. I think I'd better take one of Dr. Fowler's powders. They do help. I'll be right back. The cobbler does look delicious. I can't wait to taste it."

He piled his napkin by his plate, excused himself a second time, and went out.

"He still looks peaked," said Jean.

"Aye. He took a nasty blow; he's lucky it dinna kill

him. Poor soul, he's fidgety as a groom. He must feel an absolute jackass, catching up with that villainous scamp only to have him turn the tables and brain him. He'll need at least another week to recover completely. I do hope you dinna find it an imposition, my dear."

"Not at all. He's good company, and a perfect gentleman. But it's easy to see he's terribly upset. Getting worse every day. It's not helping him get better."

Rudy stood before the medicine cabinet mirror. He downed one, then another of Dr. Fowler's powders and appraised himself in the glass. He looked awful, felt awful, and his pride was badly bent out of shape with embarrassment. To let such a thing happen to him, a trained detective. And just as bad to have a stranger, a Pinkerton, someone who didn't even know Steinbrenner and couldn't possibly generate the hatred he harbored for him, pick up the reins and go after him. He'd never catch him, of course. Steinbrenner was too slick for anybody.

"Except me."

That was a laugh. At the moment he was in no condition to chase a crippled dog. And what if this Raider did catch him? Hauptmann Huberman would be beside himself. He'd take it as a black eye to himself! He'd given him such freedom, let him handle the case with next to no interference, provided expenses, responded promptly to his every request, filled his every need, personally arranged his traveling, hotel reservations, and the like. All he asked in return was results. The one thing, at least up to now, he could not give him. Steinbrenner appeared as safe from capture, at least by him, as he had been his first day after him. Perhaps he was going about it the wrong way. Perhaps he should be after Brünnhilde Hauser. He could use her as bait to trap him. She'd cooperate or he'd find a way to force her. Only catching her would prove just as difficult as catching him, he was sure.

Once more he examined his face, drawing first one cheek, then the other down with his hand. Sticking his tongue out. And wondered. Had he made a mistake getting into law enforcement after the war? He could have stayed in the army; they'd wanted him to. He had been present at the capture of Napoleon III. Had stood within five feet of the emperor. What an exciting three days that had been, grinding out history by the hour! And less than five months later they had marched into Paris and forced it to capitulate.

His days of glory. Why he had given up his chance to rise in rank for civilian life and detective work, for a chase that had taken him practically all over Europe, to England, to this country, was more than he could fathom now.

Perhaps the answer to his problems was simpler than he thought. As simple as the fact that Steinbrenner was the better man. More capable, efficient, intelligent, luckier. He did seem to have all the luck. His only mistake was an error in judgment: jilting his girlfriend back in Berlin. If she hadn't come to the police and told them his future plans, including a trip to the U.S., they would never have known he'd left the Continent.

For all the good the information was doing him at the moment.

He could understand why Steinbrenner would take his wallet and papers, even his gun. But his military decorations? The heartless brute. It was like filching his manhood. It was all the ready-at-hand proof he had that he was a patriot, a brave soldier and a good one. He would bet Steinbrenner never enlisted; too busy grinding out phony money and lining his pockets with the real thing.

"I hate you!"

A throat cleared behind him. The chief appeared in the glass above his right shoulder.

"Excuse me, Rudy, but Mrs. Pinkerton and I were getting worried. Are you all right? Feeling better?"

"Yes, sir. Forgive me. I am being rude to Mrs. Pinkerton, tarrying here."

"Come, we'll all have us some peach cobbler."

"Yes."

Preceding Pinkerton on their way back to the table, he made his decision. Headaches or no, he would have to leave. First thing in the morning he would borrow money from the office petty cash or whatever, tell Pinkerton he wished to buy a small gift of appreciation for Mrs. Pinkerton, buy her flowers, and use the rest to wire Berlin for money. Tell Huberman what had happened, that he knew where Steinbrenner had gotten to and was ready to pick up the chase.

The peach cobbler was delicious.

He changed his mind. He decided against deceiving the chief by asking for a loan. The following morning he approached him in his office. He was straightforward about it.

"I must wire Berlin. I will need expense money to get to Cheyenne and support myself until the case is solved."

"We'd be happy to advance you all you require. We can settle up with your superiors when the thing's wrapped up. Besides, you won't be leaving for some time. Perhaps by then Raider will have collared the blackguard for you."

Rudy sighed inwardly. He didn't want to say out loud "that's just what I'm afraid of."

"Your offer is more than generous, but I feel responsible for this mess and I think it is best if I tell Hauptmann Huberman what happened to me in New York, rather than take the chance that he learn of it from some other source. It would ease my conscience."

"You're an honorable man, Rudy." Pinkerton laid an avuncular hand on his shoulder. "As you wish. Martha-Mary, kindly take our guest here up to the telegraph room and have Walter send off his wire for him."

Rudy hung about the office all day waiting for his money to come through. Three hundred dollars arrived shortly before five. No message, no comment on his message, only the money. He was obliged to walk over to Western Union to pick it up. When he had done so, he asked for a piece of stationery and an envelope. He wrote a note to the chief.

Dear Sir,

I am leaving for Cheyenne. By the time I get there I am sure I will be completely recovered from my headaches. I am forever in your debt for your own and Mrs. Pinkerton's many kindnesses and hospitality toward me. I will send progress reports every few days as the need arises. I would appreciate it if, after reading them, you would forward copies to Hauptmann Huberman. I will contact Operative Raider as soon as I get to Cheyenne.

I feel much better today and I know I will be all right. Again, thank you both from the bottom of my heart.

> Sincerely,
> Rudolph Heinrich Fenstermacher
> Detective 1st Grade

He wrote the chief's name on the envelope, returned to the Pinkerton office building, and gave the note to the elevator man in the lobby. He tipped him and told him to hold on to the note for an hour before delivering it upstairs. On his way back to Pinkerton's house he stopped off at a florist and bought a lovely bouquet of red roses and camellias. When he got to the house he was relieved to learn that Mrs. Pinkerton was not at home. Just as well, he thought, when her daughter told him. The note to the chief explained his departure; he didn't need to go through a verbal explanation.

He packed his carpetbag and caught a hansom to La-Salle Street and the westbound train station.

Shortly after Rudy gave the envelope addressed to the chief to the elevator man, Allan Pinkerton came into William Wagner's office, deposited himself on the corner of the desk, folded his arms, and watched his superintendent work.

Wagner looked up. "I'm beginning to worry about

Raider. It's been three days and we haven't heard a whisper."

"Did you expect to? Waiting for Raider to contact the agency is like waiting for a star to fall. You can watch until your neck collapses and your eyes fall out before you see one."

"He could be lying dead in a ditch at this very moment."

"Drunk or asleep, but nae dead. He's been warned about Steinbrenner; he'll be on his guard."

"What if he didn't get the wire?"

"Why wouldn't he?"

"I don't know, but it's possible he didn't."

"Stuff ond nonsense! Your fears are groundless, man. The whole situation turned completely about face when Rudy showed up here. Thanks to him, Steinbrenner has nae idea Raider knows who he is. Raider can overpower the unsuspecting rascal and have him locked up. As I see it, Rudy solved the case for us. In his way, *he* caught the villainous wretch, using Raider as an extension of his arms, so to speak. Oh say, I like that; my capacity for mental invention is sharp as a tack."

"I wish to God we'd hear from him. And good news. If anything ever happened to him . . ."

"Guid losh, you'd think he was your own flesh and blood."

"Don't tell me you don't feel the same way."

Pinkerton stiffened, got up from the desk, walked to the door, closed it, and leaned against it. "I do, but if you ever tell him I said so, I'll deny it."

A knock sounded at his back. He turned and opened the door to Emmaline Cathcart and Rudy's message. He read it to himself.

"Guid losh!"

"What?"

"It's from Rudy. He's left town. He's on his way to join Raider and retrieve his self-esteem. Too bad he'll be too late. By the time he gets there, *if* he gets there, the bird'll be in the cage."

* * *

Fräulein Brünnhilde Hauser lay awake in her bed in her hotel room reexperiencing in mind the events of earlier in the evening. She had worked herself into a state of near distraction worrying about Gerhard, imagining all sorts of terrible things: discovery, capture, imprisonment, death— only to have him walk in as casually as if he were just returning from an errand.

Why had she worried so, after all they'd been through separately and together? Why, when he was out of her sight, did she concern herself to the point of suffering? She loved him. Adored him. If only he felt the same way toward her. If only he felt a fraction of the devotion, the tender passion she lavished on him. But he did not. It had taken her a long time to come to this admission. For two years now she had skirted it, avoided it, kept it from her with every fiber of her resolve. But continuing to was useless. He treated her like a younger sister. Her opinions held no merit in his thinking; her ideas and suggestions were invariably dismissed as worthless. He was short with her, at times even rude. Worst of all, he didn't love her. Had he ever? she wondered. Or when she believed he did, early in their relationship, was he just putting it on, pretending because he was so dependent on her for the success of his schemes? Without her he would have fallen on his face long ago. He'd be sitting in a prison cell at this very moment if she hadn't come along.

Now, in spite of all she had done for him, he was sick of her, bored with her. And so puffed up with his string of triumphs and prosperity, so proud of himself he had pushed her into the shadows. Out of his heart.

"If I was ever in it."

He refused to acknowledge her contribution, her importance, even, it seemed, her presence.

Had she been a plain-faced, insecure, even stupid drab, dull and sexless, a clinging vine, she might understand and accept his indifference. But she was beautiful! Men stared at her in the street. And she was intelligent, reliable, trust-

worthy. She was his greatest asset. And in his heart he
knew it, the ingrate!

"He's such a bastard!"

Her turmoil increased. She became upset, angry. She
got up and began pacing, muttering, complaining. It was
nearing four in the morning when she lay down again. Her
mind was made up. He could go to hell! She didn't need
him. She could go home to Germany and marry anyone she
pleased, perhaps a baron, even a count. Free of him, she
would have to fight off admirers. She would fall in love,
marry, bear a child, perhaps two, a boy and girl. And forget about him, dismiss him from her mind forever.

"The contemptible, thankless swine!"

For two years she had done everything he had asked of
her. Now he no longer asked, he ordered. And if she tried,
however politely, to raise an objection, to differ, to question his judgment, he practically flew at her! Had he not
ordered her to take the stagecoach to Pine Bluffs? She
would not. She refused. Not because it didn't make sense,
as he had explained it, but because he wanted her to.

"To the bloody devil with Pine Bluffs and stage-
coaches!"

Early tomorrow morning she would board the train for
San Francisco. Journey out of his life and back into her
own. By the time she got there she'd have come up with a
plan of her own for passing the counterfeit. Pass it, pack
up the genuine money she got in return, and be gone before
he arrived.

"I'll show him!"

"Provo, Utah! Ow! Chrissakes, stop shoutin'! I got six
blacksmiths inside my skull all beatin' on the same anvil.
Jesus, I feel rotten. Like somebody threw me up. My poor
head. Provo?"

"See for yourself."

Steinbrenner handed him the faked telegram.

"That's about forty miles south of Salt Lake City. And
ten times that from here! Ouch!"

"We can take the train. It would be only ten or twelve hours."

"I'm sicker'n four dogs. I doubt I can make it to the friggin' door."

He had started up from the bed. He sank back down, his head between his hands, his face a map of suffering. Steinbrenner studied the top of his head. It crossed his mind that he was like a bug. A beetle, a pet to amuse himself with, and when he tired of it, he would squash it flat.

"It is only a hangover. Let me help you to the window. Stand and gulp in the fresh air. It will help."

"Fresh air's bad for you. In this line I'm wha'cha call it . . . overexposed to it. What I need is a drink. Hair o' the dog. What time is it?"

"Almost eight-thirty. Raider, when I picked up that telegram last night, in talking to the clerk, he told me some interesting news. The bank teller Hampton shot himself."

"Oh, great. He was our man. Got to be. Musta figgered we were closing in. Only matter o' time before we tossed our net over him. Man couldn't stand the gaff. Poor slob."

"It appears all we have left to work with is this lead in Provo."

"Ol' Fish must be fit to bust his jewels. We best steer clear o' him. We walk in an' tell him the mint in Denver is clean, that it all happened at this end, an' that there's no way under the sun we're gonna get his money back for him, he's liable to set the dogs on us."

Steinbrenner brought out his notebook and gold pencil for the first time in many days.

"Never mind, huh? Do me a favor. Go down the street and get me a half-pint o' Taos Lightning."

"I will get you headache powders. And here, take one of my blood invigorators."

"Like hell! That'll finish me off in spades. Gimme another hour. I'll just lie down and suffer it outta me."

"Dash cold water on your face."

Raider didn't hear; he was snoring. Rudy left. Minutes later he sat in a booth alone over coffee, weighing his alternatives. He could squash the beetle right here in

Cheyenne, and thereby save him the trouble of a boring, 800-mile round trip. With Raider out of the picture, he could then board the next train to California. He checked his watch. Brünnhilde must be almost to Pine Bluffs by now. He did not know if she could make her train connection there, but wherever she made it, if he were to board his here, he would get to San Francisco before she did.

He sipped his coffee. It was hot but vile; all American coffee was vile. As was the food and wine. The beer was abominable. His thoughts went back to her. If he got there first he would wait in the station and, when she came in, follow her. Trail her about town the next couple of days and see what she did. See if she followed orders.

Beautiful Brünnhilde. For all her visible and concealed charms, she was becoming a burden lately. Carping, criticizing, second-guessing him. And constantly pestering him to take her to bed.

"Face it, Gerhard, you are sick of her. She has outlived her usefulness. She has become, alas, a pain in the neck."

Every other time she opened her lovely mouth lately it was to ask him to marry her. Demand it. Why in heaven's name did women have to be so possessive? Why did they fall in love and, when you didn't reciprocate, pester and plague you until you surrendered? Smother you with affection. All but drown you in the sticky syrup of their feelings. Disgusting! After San Francisco he would be smart to rid himself of her. Jilt her. Leave town in the dead of night. No forwarding address, no possible way for her to know where he'd gone. When they first began working together, she was a dream. Tell her what to do and she'd do it. Spendidly. A born professional. How often back then had he told himself how lucky he was to find one so lovely, so well endowed, vivacious, brainy, and cool under stress.

"Face it, Gerhard, you do not need her anymore. That is what it comes down to."

An idea exploded. She captured the hearts of poor love-lorn tellers, used them, and deserted them. Why couldn't he do the same thing to female tellers, the lovesick, lonely little things who lived by themselves and hated it? Hopeless romantics waiting in vain for their knights on white chargers, and going through the motions on the job. He certainly knew how to handle women; as capably as she did men. What did he need with her talents? Now that he compared them seriously, his own outshone hers by a wide margin.

"Gerhard, my boy, you handsome rogue, you are a damned genius!"

Raider slept until mid-afternoon. Tiring of waiting for him to wake up, Steinbrenner hooked up with a willowy brunette, took her home, and bedded her. A little before four Raider woke up. He felt better, although far from his old self. His headache had subsided, but the queasy feeling in his stomach persisted. To chase it, he would eat something and, better late than never, get his throat around that hair of the dog. Two hairs.

This decided, he got up from the side of the bed and started to dress. The faked telegram sitting on the washstand caught his eye. He read it. His conversation earlier with Rudy came back to him.

"Provo. Jesus! This is gettin' to be like chasin' a jackrabbit on sore bare feet. Don't write that down, Rudy."

He chuckled. The two of them weren't having much luck, what with Hampton shooting himself, the useless, time-consuming run down to Denver and back, the run-in with Mr. Feathers. But he was still enjoying himself. Rudy had turned out aces. He particularly appreciated his concern over the state of his hangover. He was sincere, too. He really cared how Raider felt. All in all he couldn't do enough for him. He listened to him, respected him, didn't turn every little difference of opinion into an argument like Weatherbee. Oh, he was a little quick on the trigger, maybe, but both times everything had come out okay.

"Sonovabitch, that time he shot the holdup man on the train, he near give me a heart attack. He sure has got guts, though, bless him."

He wondered where he'd gotten to. He hauled on his

boots, washed up, and went out. Across the street from the front of the hotel Rudy's front door loomed, inviting him to walk over and knock on it. In a bit, he thought. First he'd get himself something to eat and three or four hairs.

Rudy Fenstermacher stared out the window at the boring Sand Hills of western Nebraska sliding by. The relentless sameness of the landscape was enough to put one to sleep. But the conductor had just announced that Scotts Bluff was coming up. Beyond it lay Cheyenne and another in a long line of many chances to get his hands on Steinbrenner.

What was he thinking? Raider must already have him behind bars. Robbing him of his long awaited hour of glory, but he certainly shouldn't resent him for that. He was lucky to be alive.

A train hooted and hurtled past, coming from the opposite direction. He stiffened. Were Steinbrenner and Raider on it on their way back to Chicago?

"Lieber Gott, nein!"

No. Impossible. Knowing Steinbrenner as he did, even before headquarters alerted the Pinkerton to his dangerous situation, Steinbrenner and his mistress had finished with their bilking and fled the area. There'd been plenty of time.

"Which means, if that's what's happened, Raider didn't catch him. He's still free. Still mine!"

Steinbrenner's companion of the sheets got up and began putting her clothes on.

"If y'all have to go out, ah can wait for y'all to come back."

"No no."

"My, but y'all sure 'nough are in a rush, sweetheart," she purred, eyeing him hungrily.

He was sitting up. He lit a cigar. "Business."

"Ah can come on back tonight." She batted her eyes in what was too obviously intended to be enticing.

He waved away the suggestion. "Do not come here. If I complete my business, I will drop by the Pioneer."

"Ah'll be waitin' with bells on, honey."

She came to him and tried to kiss him. He gave her his cheek.

"Not now. Tonight."

She finished dressing and left. Even before he had finished playing, before climax, he decided it would be best to get rid of Raider. Then leave town. He flirted with the idea of letting him live but knowing Mr. Wild West Cowboy as he had come to over the past week, Raider would eventually have to find out who he actually was, whereupon he would take up the chase with all the persistence and single-mindedness of Fenstermacher. Rudy was amusing; he added spice to his travels and kept him on his toes. But two Rudys, coming at him from different directions or even linking up, might turn out a bit more than he could handle. Besides, Fenstermacher deserved to chase him without competition. He would never catch him, but this late in the game he had earned the right to the role of exclusive pursuer.

He checked the Gruener. Raider was probably still dead to the world in his room. Yes, by all means, get rid of him. He'd go across the street, up to his room, and render him dead to the world permanently. He wouldn't shoot him; the pistol would be a last resort. The sound of gunfire would bring everybody on the floor running. He didn't want to have to flee down the fire escape. It would be easier and safer to brain him in his sleep. Only this time make doubly sure he was dead before he left. Brünnhilde was right: he should have been more thorough with Rudy in New York.

Raider walked out of the hotel moments before Rudy left his house. On his way to the nearest restaurant Provo returned to Raider's thoughts. The telegram had sounded urgent; they really should leave tonight. Only that would mean another all-night siege of Rudy's thunderous snoring, with him winding up on the floor of the vestibule. If they caught the early-morning train they could make Provo before bedtime, and check into separate rooms.

He downed two 75-cent steaks and a pile of home fries, then repaired to the Crow Creek Saloon for an hour or so with a bottle. He found a corner table, but no sooner did he sit down and place his Stetson on the table than who should come sashaying in, all sequins and feathers, but Imogene the Popular. He groaned and reached for his hat, but when he started up, the waiter blocked his way.

"Something wrong, friend?"

"Ah . . . oh hell, I guess not. Never mind."

"What'll it be?"

"Have you gotta real, good, man-size, smooth, cheap Tennessee slop whiskey?"

"Bullard's Sour Mash. Real popular in these parts. Knock the heels off your boots."

"How much?"

"Buck a bottle."

"You call that cheap? Oh hell, I guess."

The waiter's departure opened a clear line of sight to Imogene standing talking to two men at the bar. She spotted him and came over. He sighed. It was hard to tell whether she was pleased, disappointed, or indifferent to the sight of him by her expression, but when she got to within conversation distance her first words obliterated all expectation of pleasantries.

"Well, if it isn't Mister Two-bit Tightwad himself!"

I'd tell you to shut your face, only you might crack your war paint. You got some gall callin' me a tightwad. Why don'cha hang your price list on the end o' the bed so's a body knows what he's in for?"

"Why you insulting pig!"

The waiter was bringing up his bottle. He stopped in his tracks, Bullard's in one hand, tumbler in the other, napkin over his arm. Other patrons were turning in their chairs to rubberneck. An overgrown oaf in bibs and size 18 plow boots, one of the two who had been standing at the bar with her, came pounding up. His face looked like somebody had stopped it with a shovel.

"What'd he say to you, Miss Imogene?"

Raider glared. "None o' your beeswax, Junior. Go on home an' slop your hogs. Phew, you smell like a cow barn."

Out shot a fist the size of a cantaloupe, grabbing Raider by the shirtfront, lifting him from his chair as easily as an empty sack. Everything happened at once. The chair toppled, Imogene screamed, the waiter dropped the Bullard's, shattering it, the farmer's other fist came driving at Raider's face, he jerked and ducked at the same time, took a glancing blow off the side of his head, and staggered back out of range. Sucking in a breath, he lowered and went for his gut, pounding him repeatedly as hard as he could. Hands on his hips, his glower of resentment melting into a broad smile, the giant stood his ground and took every punch with an ease that suggested someone was throwing feathers at him. Hard as he punched, Raider could not dent him. It was like belting a brick wall.

"Har, har, har, har, har!"

Again a huge fist came at Raider's face. He straightened and turned and caught it inside his shoulder. It was a pile driver. He instinctively half turned to see if it had knocked his shoulder free. Miraculously, it hadn't even fractured it. The oaf closed in, bringing his fists and his fragrance up to within two feet of Raider, by now backed against the wall. But instead of punching him, his attacker picked up the chair, lifted it overhead, and brought it straight down. His slowness of execution was all that saved Raider; he managed to slip sideways, and the chair shattered to kindling against the wall. The crowd oohed and ahhed, impressed. Sensing that if he kept retreating he'd wind up cornered and be beaten to a pulp, Raider pulled back his right and, putting everything he could into it, brought it straight up to the other's chin. The farmer jerked to one side just in time; it caught nothing but air and all but wrenched Raider's arm from his shoulder.

Demolition balls began smashing Raider's upper body and head. He weaved and ducked. Through his speedily gathering pain, he spied Sheriff Tunstall, flanked by two deputies, pushing to the forefront of the onlookers. He came striding up. By now Raider could scarcely see. He swung blindly. His fist struck bone. Imogene screamed. The crowd yelled. The attack of the steel balls stopped suddenly. Raider leaned against the wall and slowly opened his eyes. And lowered them.

At his feet, stretched out cold, was the sheriff. One of his deputies was bending over him. The other stood menacing Raider with his six-gun.

"Don't move, mister."

Raider couldn't believe his eyes. The farmer was standing a good eight feet away from him, grinning broadly. How he'd gotten there, how Tunstall had replaced him within range, all in the space of less than three seconds, he had no idea.

Tunstall was coming around. The deputy got him up to a sitting position. The sheriff rubbed his jaw gingerly.

"He did it, Mace, the tramp in the vest."

"It was a damn accident, Mace!" boomed Raider. "You saw, I was aimin' at Mister Stink there. Sonovabitch attacked me in cold blood!"

"He's a liar!" shrilled Imogene. "He struck the first blow. He was insulting me, saying the most awful things, cursing. Link heard and came to my rescue."

"That's a fact, Sheriff," said the oaf.

"That's bullshit!"

"Arrest him, Sheriff!" exclaimed Imogene.

"Just quiet down," said Tunstall wearily, continuing to rub his jaw.

"That's tellin' her, Mace," said Raider.

"You too, Pink. I'm taking you in."

"What the hell for?"

"Assault, what the hell do you think?"

"It was accidental. I was aimin' for that stinkin' slob."

"And hit me. Just come along quietly. We'll sort it all out over at the office."

"Like hell! It was an accident!"

One of the deputies had him by the arm. The other still held his gun on him. Raider shook free and confronted onlookers at the front of the crowd.

"Tell him, mister. You too. All o' you, tell him how it was."

"No need," said Tunstall. "I was here, remember? Just quiet down."

"This is bullshit!"

"And make him mind his filthy mouth, too, Sheriff!" exclaimed Imogene.

"I asked you to shut up," said Tunstall.

"You heard him," said Raider. "Damn troublemaker!"

"All right, all right. Show's over, folks. You all right, Lincoln?" Tunstall asked the farmer.

"Whatta you askin' him for? I'm the friggin' injured party!"

The sheriff ignored him. "Make way there, folks." He snaked Raider's gun out. Alton, Jethroe, bring him along."

Imogene cheered, the farmer applauded, people in the crowd leered at Raider. The waiter was down on the floor picking up the glass.

Steinbrenner knocked on Raider's door and called to him. When there was no answer, he opened it to find the room empty. He lingered briefly, looking about, then went down to the lobby to wait for him to come back from wherever he'd gone. After thirty minutes of waiting and no sign of Raider, he went out to look for him. Cheyenne boasted a population of a little over 4,000. Why it didn't have a full-time police force, he could not understand, and chalked it up to the fact that Wyoming was still a territory and yet to be blessed with some of the civilized refinements that statehood brought.

The town spread northward from Crow Creek nearly up to Sloan's Lake in labyrinthine fashion. He walked a good ten blocks looking in stores, shops, and particularly watering holes as he passed. His travels made him thirsty, and twice he stopped to refresh himself. His second stop was the Crow Creek Saloon, barely ten minutes after the fight broke up, the onlookers dispersed, and Sheriff Tunstall marched Raider off to jail, followed by Imogene, Lincoln, and a small number of the curious, all of whom the deputies sent about their business before locking Raider up.

Steinbrenner bellied up to the mahogany and ordered a

glass of Horvath's Pride of California, the only drinkable domestic wine he had been able to find since arriving in town. At the far end of the saloon Raider's waiter was picking up the pieces of the broken chair. The bartender noticed Steinbrenner noticing.

"You just missed the big to-do. Lincoln Chambers got into a squabble with some stranger over a woman. They got to going at it pretty good when Sheriff Tunstall walked in and tried to break it up. The stranger, tall drink of water with a Stetson that looked like it had been through the war and the greasiest vest on God's green earth, hauled off and clobbered the sheriff. Got himself tossed in the clink."

"He actually punched the sheriff?"

The bartender nodded. "I don't think he meant to. He was a little bleary-eyed from Link punching him."

"He took some poundin' in the face," added the waiter, coming up with the pieces of the chair.

"Stetson, dirty vest . . ." mused Steinbrenner aloud. "You did not happen to overhear his name, did you?"

They shook their heads.

"The woman jawing with him called him a two-bit tightwad."

"Did he look hung over?" Steinbrenner asked.

The waiter nodded emphatically. "He looked like he'd been drinkin' with both hands for a week."

Steinbrenner slapped his glass down so hard the contents curled upward and spilled. The quarter he dropped on the bar did not rattle to rest until the batwing doors were swinging behind him. Holding his hat on with one hand, his coattails streaming behind him, he raced up the street to the sheriff's office. In he burst. A deputy sat on a stool by the potbelly stove reading a newspaper. Tunstall sat with his feet on the desk, whistling and whittling. Most of his jaw was purple.

"Where is my partner?"

"Locked up next door. The charge is assaulting a peace officer in the performance of his duty." Tunstall did not even look up.

"It was an accident."

Tunstall looked up, snapped his knife shut, and pocketed it. "I didn't see you there."

"Can I see him?"

"I guess. Alton, mind the store."

Raider was lodged next door to the office. The dozen or so cells were not open bars but old-fashioned plate-steel cubicles. Each door boasted a six-inch-square window with small bars at eye level. Curious faces appeared at their windows as Raider's filled his. He was furious.

"Where you been!" he boomed at Tunstall. "Hasn't this farce gone far enough? You've had your friggin' vengeance. We're even. Besides, if you think about it, you're only makin' yourself look foolish. Everybody there saw it was an accident. Unintentional. You know it was. How's it look for the number-one badge in town to be such a sorehead? That's what you're bein'."

"Calm down," said Steinbrenner. "He does have a point, Sheriff."

"And I've got a jaw that feels dislocated. You pack some wallop," he said to Raider.

"I was only defendin' myself. Damn it, you saw!"

"Are you going to carry on like this all night?"

"I'm gonna carry on right up to and into the damn court. Which is where you an' me gotta wind up if you don't get wise to yourself. I ask you, how's it gonna look you gettin' up on the stand testifyin' I cold-cocked you and then, bein' under oath as you'll be, you gotta admit it was accidental? Judge'll toss it out before you can get up from the chair. And right there is where your big trouble starts. I'll sue you into the poor farm for false arrest! I'll—"

"*Halts maul!*" boomed Steinbrenner.

Both gaped at him.

"I mean shut up! You talk and talk and talk and talk . . ."

Raider looked painfully hurt.

"Amen to that," rasped Tunstall. He got the key ring down from its peg and unlocked the door. "Get out of here. Get our of my ears, out of my life, out of town. The two of you!"

"We're leavin'," rejoined Raider. "Our boy's flown the coop. Been seen in Provo."

"Good. Go bend a few Mormon ears. They'll give that red rag of yours two days, then run you off to Idaho."

They stood outside. Raider's leer was unmistakably one of triumph. "Guess I talked my way outta that one, eh, partner?"

Steinbrenner threw up his hands. They walked off. Raider resumed babbling. He changed the subject from his deliverance from durance vile to Provo.

"Nice town. You'll like it. Insane asylum's there, you know. We'll leave first train tomorrow. We head straight across Wyoming, cross the border just below Randolph, and when we get to Echo City, change to the southbound train for Provo. If we can make the connection fast enough, we can make town before bedtime."

For no particular reason, they headed toward the train station. Raider pointed this out to him. "We can stop by and ask when the first train tomorrow is."

Steinbrenner only half listened to his rambling, preoccupied as he was with when and where he should dispatch him, convinced that it would best be done before they boarded the train.

He stopped suddenly, seized Raider's arm, gaped, and pointed. "Look!"

"What? I don't see nothin'. Except that skinny, pasty-faced guy with the carpetbag."

"It's him! F . . . Steinbrenner!"

"Whatta you talkin' about. What would he be doin' comin' back here?"

"It's him. No mistake!"

"Holy. . . ."

CHAPTER TEN

Steinbrenner pulled Raider under an overhang into shadow. They watched the man with the carpetbag cross the street and move away from them.

"What fantastic luck!" boomed Steinbrenner.

"Ssssh, Chrissakes, he'll hear you. He sees you, he'll rabbit. Stay here outta sight, I'll go collar him."

"No, no, no! I will. I must! I have been waiting for this moment for three years. You or no one else can deprive me of my triumph!"

"I guess. Hey, goodbye, Provo. Go ahead, I'll be right behind you."

"No. Go back to the sheriff's and wait for me."

"You kiddin'? He'd like to see my face again about as much as Steinbrenner wants to see you. I'll wait here. Go grab him. Come back this way—you gotta to get to the jug."

Steinbrenner started away before he could finish. Raider watched him break into a run and speculated on what was passing through his mind. It *was* his "moment of triumph." After three fruitless years, he finally had him in his sights.

97

"Go get him, Rudy boy, more power to you."

One, then the other, rounded the corner, vanishing from sight. Raider waited. Across the street Imogene walked by in the company of a heavyset older man. She was so busy talking to him she didn't notice Raider. He was tempted to call out to her. All sorts of snide remarks whizzed through his mind, but he held his tongue.

He turned and looked in the store window. It was a pharmacy. A large poster dominated the window:

DR. C.V. GIRARD'S

GINGER BRANDY

A Certain Cure for Cholera, Colic Cramps,
Dysentery, Chills & Fever,
is a delightful
and healthy beverage

FOR SALE HERE

Sir James Clarke's Celebrated Female Pills, Hoofland's German Bitters, and dozens of other patent medicines were on display. He also spied Reilly's Pomatum Mustache Wax. He flirted with the idea of buying a bar to present to Rudy when he returned with his captive, a sort of celebration gift, but then noted that the price was an exorbitant ten cents. He was tempted to step inside and tell the pharmacist that Reilly's was available across the street for eight cents.

He glanced up the street. There was no sign of Rudy or the man with the carpetbag. It crossed his mind that Rudy might have run into trouble. Steinbrenner was desperate. He'd fight like a wildcat to avoid capture.

"Comin', Rudy."

Away he sprinted. He tore around the corner. There was no sign of either of them. He ran a block, crossed the street, and was halfway to the next cross street when he stopped short at the sight of the carpetbag lying on the sidewalk. Down at the shadowed end of an alley he spied

Rudy, gun in hand, aiming at the prostrate form of his quarry.

"Rudy! Hey!" Raider retrieved the bag and ran up to them.

Steinbrenner had turned when Raider called. He now turned back to his captive. "On your feet."

Raider set the bag down and knelt. "He's out cold."

"He put up a fight, I had to hit him."

"You hit him good, he'll be out for an hour."

"I did not realize."

"Don't know your own strength, I know." He picked up the bag. "I'll take his feet, you grab the heavy end. And thanks."

"For what?"

"Savin' us both another wild goose chase. Provo."

Tunstall locked the cell door and confronted Raider and Steinbrenner. "He's got some nasty bump over the eye. There's even a little blood. He needs tending to. I'll send one of the boys to get Doc Friedland. I have to fill out the arrest report. What's the charge?"

"Counterfeiting, murder, attempted murder, flight to escape capture and prosecution," said Steinbrenner. "Take your pick."

"How long will you want me to hold him?"

"Until tomorrow mornin'," said Raider. "We'll be takin' him back to Chicago."

"Whatever you do," said Steinbrenner, "do not let him get away. When the doctor goes in, either you or one of your deputies must stand outside here and keep an eye on him. He is very clever, very resourceful. He could pretend to be still unconscious and overpower the doctor."

"Don't worry," said Tunstall in a somewhat testy tone. "Nobody gets away from us. Besides, the shape he's in, he can't get ten feet. How come you hit him so hard?"

"How come?" Raider repeated.

"Self-defense. He saw me. He must have heard me behind him. He dropped his bag and ran."

Raider frowned. "Into a blind alley?"

Steinbrenner shrugged. "He panicked. I chased him. Before I could get my gun out, he attacked me. He went for my throat. I hit him with my fist."

"You got some sledgehammer there," said the sheriff, looking at Raider as he did. "Let's go back to the office."

Steinbrenner and Raider stood outside watching Deputy Jethro Miner go off after the doctor.

"I am going home and pack my things," said Steinbrenner. "I suggest you do the same."

"I got nothin' much. Only take me a minute. No hurry." Raider scanned the sky. "Gettin' dark fast. You must be feelin' pretty good. Congratulations."

"Thank you. It is amazing, I have been after him so long, it seems a century. And to come so close so many times. To have him practically walk into my arms like this seems so—how do you say it?—anticlimactic."

"Yeah, well, main thing is you got him. Boy, he sure don't look like any international big-time paperhanger. Looks more like a clerk. How's about we go hoist a couple to celebrate?"

"Later. Now I must pack."

"Okay."

Steinbrenner walked briskly away. Raider followed him with his eyes. What was he in such a hurry for? he wondered, he had all night to pack. And how come he was so antsy all of a sudden? With the load finally off his shoulders, he should be so relaxed he could hardly stand. He *talked* like he was relaxed and relieved, he just didn't act that way. Maybe because it had happened so fast, and been wrapped up so fast, it hadn't had time to sink in yet.

"Could be."

He wondered, too, why Steinbrenner had come back to Cheyenne. What for? He'd finished up here: planted his queer, collected his genuine, and left town. Why come back and risk being fingered?

Up the street he spied the deputy approaching hurriedly in the company of a little man in a floppy parson's hat and swallowtail coat. He wore a full white beard and carried a physician's satchel. He barely came up to the deputy's shoulder.

The deputy hailed Raider as they came up to him. "Mister, this here's Doc Friedland. This is the Pinkerton man I was tellin' ya about, Doc."

"Good. Where's the patient?"

They went inside with him. The prisoner was still unconscious. Jethro unlocked the cell door and left.

"This boy looks in a bad way," said Friedland. "What happened, house fall on him?"

Raider explained, then: "Patch him up best you can, okay? He's got a long trip ahead of him. We leave for Chicago in the morning."

"We'll see. Look, he's coming around. Easy, son."

"Hey, we gotta leave tomorrow."

"Do me a favor, okay? Shut up and back off. Give me room to operate."

"Operate!"

"Oh, for pity's sakes!"

Rudy began mumbling.

"What's he sayin'? What's he sayin'?"

"Gibberish. Give him a chance. I've a better idea. You go back to the sheriff's office and wait for me. Don't worry, I know how to lock the door."

"Just don't forget to."

Friedland glared disdainfully.

"I gotta question him."

"Out!"

Raider left.

He sat on a stool in Tunstall's office, waiting. "That sawbones reliable? He won't walk out and leave his cell door open or nothin'?"

"Hardly."

"Just askin'."

"Where's your sidekick?"

Raider told him.

"Well, we close up shop in about fifteen minutes. There's not much sense you hanging around."

"You gonna put a guard on his nibs?"

"He's locked up. His cell door's locked, and the side door, and the front. Don't be such a worrywart."

They waited with Jethro. The deputy got out a checkerboard and invited Raider to play. He declined. Tunstall resumed whittling, scattering chips all over the floor. Raider had no idea what he was making, but whatever it was he didn't seem to be much of a wood carver.

Doc Friedland came in and pulled up the last available stool. "Concussion."

"My partner only hit him with his fist."

"So *he* says. Looks more like a gun butt to me."

"He still gibberishin'? He say anythin'?"

Jethro stopped playing checkers with himself and Tunstall stopped whittling.

"Nothing that makes sense. Allan Pinkerton."

"The chief."

"I gather he was a house guest of his."

"That's bullshit."

"He talked about having dinner with Chief Pinkerton and his wife. Leaving the table, going to the bathroom for a headache powder."

"That's just dizzy talk. Anythin' else?"

"That's about it. He'd mumble, then he'd sort of fade out. He'll come around. Oh, there was one other thing, something about being hit on the head."

"Which is why we called you."

"I mean before. He mentioned New York."

Raider furrowed his brow in thought.

"Mean anything?" Tunstall asked.

"It sure is confusin' as hell. "Lemme go talk to him."

"Not now," said Friedland sternly. "He needs to rest. I hope he'll sleep through the night. I'll drop by first thing tomorrow."

"We're leavin' early."

"He's not. He's not going anywhere till I say so."

"Oh for Chrissakes, he's not hurt that bad."

"I told you: concussion."

"Lemme go talk to him before he falls asleep. I just

wanta ask him a couple questions. It won't hurt him none."

Friedland jerked a thumb at Raider and addressed the sheriff. "Keep him out of there, Mason. I'm holding you responsible." He glanced back at Raider. "Time enough to talk to him in the morning."

"Okay, okay, no need to get hard-nosed."

Friedland stood up to his full five-foot-three and stretched and retrieved his satchel. "I've given him a pain-killer and a sedative to help him sleep. See that he's not disturbed. Good night."

He walked out.

"Gimme a break, Mace, gimme two minutes," said Raider.

"Sit down and forget it. Jethro, get a blanket from the cabinet and take it next door for him. Then go on home. What's bugging you, Raider? Why do you have to talk to him? What about?"

"This. None of it figures, and he's the only one with the answers. Think about it. Steinbrenner and his accomplice, the woman, paper the town."

"Poor Charlie Hampton papered it for 'em, it appears," Tunstall said.

"Whatever. She skins out. I mean she's sure not around, it only makes sense she pulled out. Steinbrenner was here. At least it seems he was. Everything points to it. He leaves, then turns right around and comes back. Then all this mumblin' besides—about bein' the chief's house guest, goin' to the bathroom."

Tunstall nodded. "Getting hit on the head in New York."

"That too."

"I'll admit it's confusing, but it can all wait till morning. Let's get out of here." The sheriff rubbed his tender, badly bruised chin. "I'll let you buy me a snort. Peace offering."

"Some other time. I gotta go catch up with my partner. Find out more about Steinbrenner."

He went to Rudy's house. He knocked and knocked, but there was no answer. It occurred to him that Rudy might have finished packing and gone across the street to the hotel to find him. He looked in the lobby, but there was no sign of him. "Now where the hell has he got to?"

It was still early, the night people not yet out in force. Stores and other businesses were in darkness, but the saloons, dance halls, and other establishments were brightly lit. He stood in front of the hotel, ruminating. A wagonload of manure trundled by. Raider grimaced and held his nose till it passed. He was bringing his hand back down when a shot rang out. The driver and everybody on both sides of the street froze in a tableau, reacted, then resumed what they were doing.

The shot had come from the vicinity of the sheriff's office. One shot, muffled.

"From behind it."

He hurried over. Pedestrians had stopped and were talking about it, but none made a move to investigate. The office was in darkness. The front door was locked. He hurried around back. It too was locked. He went next door to the jail. A barrel lay on its side near the wall under one of the two cell windows that looked out on the backyard. Raider's well-honed instinct for trouble caused him to stiffen. He righted the barrel, got up on it, and peered through the barred window.

"Sonovabitch!"

Steinbrenner lay abed, half covered by the blanket, moonlight illuminating the scene. He had been shot through the heart.

CHAPTER ELEVEN

Raider found the sheriff holding down a table at the back in the Pioneer. He was alone. He listened in awe to Raider.

"Is he dead?"

"He looks fairly dead," growled Raider. "Come on."

Minutes later Tunstall inserted the key in the cell door and looked inside. "No need to check him. Man's dead as a fish. Who the hell would want to kill him? The woman, you think?"

"His accomplice? I dunno. I really gotta find Rudy. Somethin' stinks here."

"Check all the saloons, why don't you."

"Mmmmm."

Raider had heard him, but did not budge.

"What now?" Tunstall asked.

"Really stinks. To high heaven. It just don't add up. Lemme in there."

"Okay. Okay."

Raider went through the dead man's pockets. He couldn't find a wallet, but he did find over $260 in cash. Nothing else. Not so much as lint in his pockets.

"Crazy," he murmured to Tunstall, who stood patiently watching him. "No identification."

"He was a wanted man. He probably decided not to carry anything that would give away his true identity."

"I'm beginnin' to wonder what that is. Wanted or not, everybody carries somethin' with their name on it. And he's got nothin' besides—no old telegrams, letters, even a slip of paper, even his punched ticket. We did spot him walkin' away from the station. Most conductors punch your ticket and hand it back."

"Probably threw it away. Most people do when they've finished their trip." Tunstall nodded, agreeing with himself.

"Wish he'd kept his. It'd say where he came from."

"Is that important?"

"I dunno. I really don't know nothin'. That's what's buggin' me. Do me a favor, Mace, get hold of Doc Whiskers, get him back here, an' have him dig the slug out."

"Can't it wait till morning?"

"Tonight, please. Right away. I gotta go."

"What do you expect the bullet to tell you?" Tunstall frowned.

"I dunno. We'll just have to see."

"Where to now?"

"To find Rudy."

"I just told you, make the rounds of the saloons."

"Is there any train outta here this late, do you think?"

"Search me. There has to be a milk train, but that wouldn't be till real late. Want me to check it for you?"

"I'll check. You go get the doc."

Raider hurried to the depot and wondered as he did why he was doing so. Why would Rudy leave town without him? He wouldn't. Still, no harm in checking before he started on the watering holes. He'd certainly get no answers now from Steinbrenner. Maybe Rudy could help clear things up, solve all the problems.

"On the other hand, what if it turns out he's the problem?"

One aspect of the thing nagged at him more than all the others combined: Friedland's telling them Steinbrenner had mumbled about visiting Allan Pinkerton's home, even to being his and Jean's house guest. Why would he say such a thing, even if he'd stopped off in Chicago, which seemed highly doubtful, if it wasn't true? If Raider were him, he'd have given it a wide berth, would have kept away from all big cities.

Was he just mouthing off, showing off? Pulling the leg of whoever was listening? Not in the shape he was in. Come to think of it, he didn't look very healthy at their first sight of him arriving in town, even before Rudy hit him.

He thought back to the carpetbag lying on the sidewalk, his glancing into the alley and discovering Rudy and him lying in a heap. Rudy had had his gun on him. Had just finished knocking him cold, had to know he did, and yet there he stood, gun in hand, ordering him to get up.

Or was he pretending to when he arrived? For his benefit? Now that he thought about it, he didn't *look* like he was ordering him to his feet, despite his saying it. The way he stood, the way he held the Gruener, it looked more like he was about to plug him.

What was unusual about that? He certainly must hate him enough to shoot him. Could have been planning to all along. He wouldn't be the first lawman to chase a criminal for weeks and months—years, actually—and be so bitter, so furious when he did finally catch up that nothing would serve but that he finish him off then and there. He remembered now Rudy's mentioning that he'd gone for his throat. It could be he'd gotten hold and got in one good squeeze of his windpipe before Rudy clobbered him. That could have been the last straw. Could have, would have, could have, would have . . .

"Where are you?"

The station platform was deserted. The skinny, pock-marked, rheumy-eyed old man sitting behind the ticket window bars was reading the schedule. Raider interrupted and described Rudy.

"Ain't seen him."

"When's the next train?"

"The ten-fifty-eight for Laramie, then no more till four-forty-two goin' the same way."

"What about the other direction?"

"Which? East? North? South to Denver?"

"Jesus, how many are there?"

"Only one, headin' down to Denver. Let's see." He squinted at the schedule.

"Never mind. Look, I'm . . ." He showed his I.D. "I'm workin' with the sheriff. I'll have him send over a deputy to hang around and keep his eyes peeled for this fella, okay?"

"Whatcha want him so bad for? What's he done?"

"Nothin', maybe, I just gotta find him. Matter of life an' death."

"He murder somebody?"

Raider stiffened. "Could be, old-timer, could be."

He thanked him and left to begin searching the town. Once, years ago, he had been in New Orleans with Doc Weatherbee between assignments. They had gotten tickets to an outdoors bare-knuckle fight between Battling Billy Bosditch and some Cuban, Jose or Pedro Something. He couldn't recall his last name. A round ended when one or the other was knocked down. Up to the fourteenth or fifteenth round it was all Battling Billy, but from then on the tide turned. Completely.

It had turned here. Upon reflection, his discovery of the prisoner shot dead in his cell had been the turning point. From then on—searching his pockets, recalling his babbling as reported by the doctor, his own failure to find Rudy—the tide had turned against his partner, just the way it had turned against Battling Billy. Bosditch had ended up being knocked cold. At the moment Rudy was on the ropes and ready to go down. Hurrying up the street, Raider thought one last time that he could be wrong. The least he could do was give him the benefit of the doubt until he was absolutely certain he was the problem.

"Findin' you could help."

Tunstall had worked fast. The light was on in the jail. A

chorus of snoring sounded. The cell door was open. Friedland was working on the body.

"Nothing yet," said the sheriff. "Anything with you?"

"He didn't leave town. Yet. Do me a favor. Wake up one of your boys and get him over to the depot to keep an eye out. Any of 'em know him by sight?"

Tunstall chuckled. "No need. I'll just tell whoever I get to look for those outrageous mustachios. What are you up to?"

"Makin' the rounds, what do you think?"

"Hold everything," said the doctor. "Pay dirt." He straightened and held up a badly mashed slug.

Raider ran over to him. "Give it here."

"You mind if I wipe it off?"

"No time." Raider snatched it from his grasp. It was badly mangled. "Musta hit bone. Look at it, Mace."

"Looks like any other to me."

"Look close, look at the size of it. It's no forty-five, not a forty-four. It's big as a cannonball, Chrissakes. You got a chart of some kind in your office you can measure it?"

"No."

"Never mind."

He got out his gun. Friedland shrank back at the sight of it. Raider broke it and pulled a cartridge out of the chamber.

The sheriff held them up and compared them. "Could be a nine millimeter."

"Could be eleven."

"No such animal."

"Maybe not in the U.S., but over to Europe. Like Germany. Unless I'm dead wrong or drunk as a hoot owl, that came from his Gruener."

"Your partner?"

"Amen. Whatta you think, Doc, is this eleven millimeter?"

"I wouldn't know. I don't use 'em, I just dig 'em out. Why, would you believe I even got up from the table in the middle of my supper to answer the call to duty?"

"Sorry about that," mumbled Raider. "Coulda been worse. You coulda been asleep."

"And he could have shot him in the morning after breakfast."

"I'll go get Jethro to cover the train station," said Tunstall. "Where will you be?"

"I got an idea. Figure Sixteenth Street is the middle street in town. I'll take the south half, you take the north. If you find him, take him at gunpoint if he makes you."

Skepticism flooded the sheriff's face, stretching all the way down to his bruise. "You don't actually think I'm going to find him. Or you. If he killed Steinbrenner..."

"He *is* Steinbrenner! That fella there is Rudy, I mean the real Rudy Fensterwhatever. I been workin' elbow to elbow with the real Steinbrenner all along, thinkin' he was Rudy."

"How could you let him dupe you?" asked the doctor.

"He didn't, goddamn it. He could *prove* he was Rudy! *His* wallet. *His* I.D. Chrissakes, he was even wearin' his war medals on his long johns shirt."

Friedland eyed him with an incredulous look. "Come now."

"I saw 'em. He showed me! C'mon, let's go find him, Mace. I'll start now. You go shake out your deputy, send him over to the depot, an' you start combin' the north side up to the lake."

Tunstall gestured patience. "Slow down. Think about it. If, as you say, your Rudy *is* this Steinbrenner and this poor soul here is the real Rudy and Steinbrenner shot him, would he hang around town? Would you?"

Raider's response came out in a tone of desperation. "We can at least look."

"Nobody's asking me," said the doctor, "but if I were the killer, I wouldn't count on any train this late in the day. I'd hightail it to the nearest stable, grab the first animal with four sound legs, and head for the hills."

"That's it!" boomed Tunstall. "That's exactly what he did."

Raider sparked to the idea. "How many horse peddlers you got in town? Never mind, we'll each take half."

"No, no, no. We'll take the one closest to the scene of the crime, right?"

"Waste of time," interposed Friedland airily. "They're all closed for the day."

"So we'll go to their houses and—"

"Won't do you any good," said Friedland. "Remember, it was already dark when he shot our friend here. My guess is he set off for the nearest stable, broke in, and took his pick."

"That's just what he did!" Raider nodded vigorously and clapped his hands in a way that suggested he'd just discovered gold. "Why else did he run back to his place to pack after we brought the real Rudy in here? Told me he was gonna. I wondered why he was in such a rush to—"

"Now you know," said Friedland.

"I figured it was for us to leave in the mornin' for Chicago."

"But you just said—"

"Hey, anybody ever tell you you got a big mouth for someone supposed to work with his head and hands?" Raider glared.

"Hey, anybody ever tell you you shoot from the hip like nobody I've ever met? Or ever wanted to? Try closing your big yap long enough to stop and think and sort things out sensibly."

"Aw, shut your face!"

"Cut it out, both of you!" growled Tunstall.

"I will if he will, but if he won't . . ." growled Friedland.

"Oh shut up! Doc, I appreciate everything you've done for us. Especially on such short notice. Would you mind one last thing? Would you see to the body here? I've got my hands full. And don't forget to send us your bill." Raider glared.

"Don't worry, I plan to. I'll collect the corpse in the morning."

Friedland wiped his hands with a reasonably clean cloth, rolled his sleeves down, donned his swallowtail coat, snapped his bag shut, and put on his hat. "Now, if you boys don't mind, I'll go home and have my dessert. Apple pie with Wisconsin cheese."

Out he went, flinging them a wave with his last words.

As the door closed behind him, Raider said, "So what are we standin' round for? Let's get over to the closest stable and put the owner to work. He can check his stock in two shakes."

"Wait, wait, wait. Suppose we do just that. Suppose we find he stole a horse. Where'll that get you? You think he left a paper trail or something for you to follow?"

"Hey, he's carryin' two big, heavy suitcases. He'd have his hands full luggin' them on horseback. If he stole a horse, he'd steal a buggy, too. Must have."

"I didn't know about the suitcases."

"Hoofprints might be tough to follow, but buggy wheels are somethin' else. If we do spot some, they'll tell us which direction he took off in, right?"

"Perhaps."

Jake Kinsella had gone to bed early. They awakened him from a sound sleep and practically pulled him bodily out of the house. In nightcap, matching striped nightshirt, and floppy slippers, lantern in hand, he accompanied them to his stables. Raider whispered to Tunstall that Kinsella's mood was as foul as his breath.

"Couldn't you two check the place without rousting me out? You're the law, Tunstall."

"I'd rather not break it by breaking in, Jake. Sorry for the inconvenience, but this really is an emergency."

"Isn't it always?"

The front-door padlock had not been tampered with. They trudged down the side of the stable to the rear. The thief had broken in through the double doors in back.

"Sweet Jesus!" Jake boomed. "Look at that! I just laid out six bucks for a new Holton six-lever padlock, new hinges up and down. Damn!"

One door stood ajar, hanging awkwardly, the top hinge snapped cleanly in two, the padlock broken. Tunstall and Kinsella went inside. Raider scanned the ground for tracks. Inside, Kinsella swore vilely.

Tunstall came out. "He's missing a bay gelding and a brand-new spindle-body road wagon."

"Look at these tracks." Raider pointed from the ground westward. "Laramie, you betcha."

Kinsella came out scowling. "This night's work has cost me a pretty penny, the thieving scum! That vehicle was brand-new; I just took shipment yesterday." He smirked. "Still, if he had to take something, better he take it. The left rear wheel was giving me fits. Wobbled on its axle. I tightened the fit, but it's still not right."

"You saying it could fall off?" Tunstall asked.

"I don't know about that."

"Would it act up right away?" Raider asked.

"That either."

"It couldn't have." Tunstall shook his head. "If it did there'd be more tracks. He'd wheel around and come back for another one."

Raider nodded.

"Can I go home to bed now?" Kinsella rasped.

Raider frowned. "And leave your door like it is?"

"It can wait till morning. Folks in this town don't break into livery stables in the dead of night. This had to be the scum you boys are looking for."

"It is," said Raider. He lifted his glance and looked off toward Laramie. "How far do you think, Mace?"

"Over forty miles. But he may not have gone that far. There's Borie, Granite, Tie Siding, and Redbuttes before Laramie."

"Laramie's where he's headin', I feel it in my bones. And we got one big help on our side."

"Those mustachios of his."

"Right. They stand out like a red flag."

"Not if he shaves them off."

"He won't. They're the crownin' glory of his face. He's vain as a peacock about 'em. He'd no more shave 'em off than cut off his right hand."

"You heading out?"

"Hey, Kinsella, hold on a shake. Rent me a mount, okay? A good one, and the cheapest Texas saddle you got."

CHAPTER TWELVE

The train carrying the lovely Brünnhilde Hauser and her packet of newly printed bogus ten-dollar bills came blowing and clanging into Union Station in the City by the Bay. The 45-hour trip over the Rockies through the Wasatch Mountains, by the Great Salt Lake, over the desert of the same name, through the mountains of northern Nevada, across the Black Rock Desert, over the Sierra Nevada Mountains of California, through the Sacramento Valley, around the northern reaches of the Diablo Range, and to her destination had given the lady a long time to reflect upon her immediate future and her future after she and San Francisco parted company.

If anything, by the time she arrived she felt even more determined to break with Steinbrenner. And more out of pique than for any other reason, she was equally determined to devise a different stratagem to pass the bogus $30,000. No lovestruck, cow-eyed nobody of a teller to dupe, use, and abandon this time!

Winding through the Rockies, she considered the idea of splitting the money into six packets of $5,000 each, depositing them in six different banks, and two days later withdrawing genuine money. But by the time the train passed through Salt Lake City, she rejected the plan as too complicated and too risky. Puffing over the Sierra Nevadas, she hit upon an inspired idea.

The train shuddered to a stop. The conductor voiced instructions to follow the ramp up to the station. She crossed the crowded lobby to the main entrance. She was tired from lack of sleep, but her heart was high, and the sight of the glorious sun and the bustling city raised it even higher. She was, she told herself, on the threshold of the greatest, most exciting adventure of her life.

The sidewalks were as mobbed as the station. Even before disembarking she had decided not to register at the Crocker House as Steinbrenner had instructed. She would choose her own hotel. From now on she would do all her own choosing!

But climbing into a hansom cab at the curb, she changed her mind. She would register at the Crocker House after all, only under an assumed name. She told the driver where to take her and settled back to think up a name. Victoria had a nice ring to it; it was regal-sounding, as regal as Queen Victoria. Much better than Brünnhilde, which conjured up the image of a buxom, overweight opera singer. Victoria ah . . . von Werder—after Count von Werder, Prussian hero of the recent war.

Ten minutes later she stood in the sedate and dignified surroundings of the Crocker House lobby, under a plaster ceiling cluttered with flying cherubs supported by solid oak beams thirty-five feet tall. The bellboy behind her, she crossed an enormous Smyrna rug, passing leather gents' spring-seat easy chairs separated by potted palms twenty feet tall.

Her suite was on the top floor overlooking the bay. It was an extravagance she owed herself, beautifully furnished in gilded imitation Louis XIV furniture with capacious maroon velvet drapes and a canopy bed resplendent with hand-embroidered rosebuds in profusion, a bed fit for a queen. What an improvement on the hotel room in

Cheyenne! But then what an improvement San Francisco was over that rustic backwater.

As she bathed and changed into a sedate-looking, emerald-green silk frock, she reminded herself that she had only seven days to plant the money, total the profits, and get out. By now Steinbrenner, with or without the Pinkerton, must be in Provo.

It was nearing the noon hour. She was hungry, but first things first. With this in mind, she left the hotel to search for employment.

In a bank.

As a teller. Or whatever other job they had to offer involving contact with money in large amounts.

The small brass sign turned to face the visitor's chair in Vice-President Hannibal Macomber's office in the rear of the Union Trust caught a sunbeam through the window. It bounced off and struck her in the eyes. Vice-President Hannibal Macomber noticed her wince and chivalrously repositioned the sign.

"Have you ever worked in a bank before?" he asked.

He was old. She guessed he must be close to seventy. Old enough to be attracted to her, indeed to be overwhelmed by her beauty and succumb to her request for employment. He was also distressingly homely; he resembled a pig. That too could help. With that face he was undoubtedly a bachelor.

"In Germany."

She falsified credentials off the top of her head and was surprised at how authentic they sounded.

"Excellent. Very impressive. And do you have any letters of recommendation?"

She started slightly. She hadn't even thought about that. "I . . . I'm afraid not. But I wouldn't want anyone to take me at my word. That would be unfair. I'd be happy to work for a week on a trial basis without pay. No obligation whatsoever on the part of the bank. To prove my worth."

"Mmmmm." He was visibly unimpressed. "Is there anyone in town who would be willing to vouch for your, ahem . . . your character. Nothing personal, understand, but in banking we must be extremely careful."

"I can assure you, sir, I am scrupulously honest."

"I'm sure you are, Miss . . ."

"Von Werder."

"But we do require character references. If it were up to me, in this case I might make an exception, but . . . Isn't there anyone?"

"I know nobody here. I just arrived this morning."

He stood up, signaling an end to the interview. She consciously suppressed a "that's that" shrug.

"I'm sorry. Please understand," he said.

"Of course. Thank you for giving me your time. Unfortunately, banking is the only business I know."

"But surely you can put your experience to work in a store or some other business. As a bookkeeper, for instance. Qualified, experienced bookkeepers are always in demand."

"Yes, well, thank you and good day."

She walked out, leaving him slightly startled. Outside, she decided it wasn't going to be as easy as she had surmised. Without references, without at least one letter of recommendation. . . . Perhaps she could falsify both. No. Whoever she presented them to, along with her fanciful tale of her experience in banking in Germany, would only check their authenticity the moment she was out the door.

She'd simply have to turn up the glow a notch—present herself at her loveliest, most seductive, and charming.

All thoughts of Vice-President Hannibal Macomber vanished at the sight of Vice-President Anson Sterling. He welcomed her into his office, which was smaller than Macomber's but tastefully appointed. Sterling looked to be a third the older man's age. He was handsome. He was beautiful. Her heart skipped one beat, then another when he shook her hand and held the chair for her. His dark red hair rose a good two inches above his brow. He wore it long and full, with curls at the back of his neck. His blue eyes sparkled mischievously. In profile he looked even handsomer than full-face. A Greek god! And what a physique! It actuated goose pimples. Taller than Gerhard by a good three inches, he looked as if he could pick him up with one hand. He was suave, a perfect gentleman, exuding breeding. His voice was low and sexy, and early on she saw that he had a way of focusing his eyes on hers, seizing and holding them.

They sailed through the formalities. It took all of three minutes.

"We do need someone in the vault." He winked and grinned. "Can you count?"

"Carefully and without a mistake. Banks in Germany do not tolerate careless mistakes."

"Banks in America feel the same way," he said and chuckled. "The pay is eight dollars a week. Report to Mrs. Tchakarides in the morning. Eight o'clock. She'll show you the ropes. Welcome to the Crocker Bank."

"I'm hired?"

"It does sound like it."

"Oh, thank you! Thank you! I won't disappoint you, I promise."

He leaned over the desk and brought his face within a few inches of hers. "Neither, Miss von Werder, will I."

CHAPTER THIRTEEN

Raider rode at full gallop for better than thirty minutes, tripling, even quadrupling his quarry's pace. He followed the tracks, losing them, finding them again, crossing his fingers that the wobbly wheel would perform up to his hopes and add a second stroke of luck to his discovery of Steinbrenner's route. Perhaps, he speculated, the wheel would fall off and drop the unsupported corner of the glorified buggy hard against a rock—knock the axle end out of shape, make it impossible to restore the wheel, even if it came to rest in the ditch without breaking. If that happened, Steinbrenner would have no choice but to bareback the horse to the nearest town, lugging the cumbersome suitcases. Raider had wondered when the two of them left Chicago why he packed such large luggage. Now he could guess what he was carrying besides his clothing, toothbrush, and mustache trimmer.

Mr. Mustache was very patient and very careful in everything he did. Nine out of ten men would have fled by train. He obviously planned to, but had the foresight to sneak in a twist designed to mislead any possible pursuers. A monkey wrench in the machinery of Raider's guesswork.

Raider could feel the horse beginning to tire. He slackened the pace and squinted through the darkness ahead. The road stretched straight as a ribbon as far as he could see. No sign of anybody. The tracks reappeared; when visible they were easy to follow. And few buggies traveled the Laramie road, the train being so convenient and frequent during the day. He was passing through an area thick with trees, then out of them and through tiny, almost totally darkened Borie. He slowed to look for road wagons in alleys, parked alongside buildings, but did not see any type of vehicle parked outdoors. It was the same in Granite and Tie Siding.

His thoughts flew back to Cheyenne, the railroad depot, and his brief conversation with the old-timer at the ticket window. The 10:58 and 4:42 were the only two trains, making them roughly 11:58 and 5:42 on the Laramie schedule. Even driving like the wind, Steinbrenner could never make the 11:58.

What time had he left town? Doc Friedland had mentioned it was already dark out when Rudy had been shot. Somewhere around nine? He must have been all packed and ready to leave before coming to the rear of the jailhouse. Perhaps he'd broken into the stable even before coming. At that, even if he'd waited till after the deed, it would only be fifteen minutes at the most before he was on the road.

"About nine-fifteen."

He lost the tracks in a jumble of larger ones: the tracks of two big farm wagons coming out of a side road ahead, one following the other, obliterating the road wagon's skinny tracks. But passing the entrance to the side road a mile farther on, he picked up the stolen road wagon's tracks again. The moon hung fat and shining, lighting the rugged landscape like day. The weather was mild, with a whisper of a breeze curling down from the summits of the southern end of the Laramie Range. Rocky country this; the farther one moved westward, the ruggeder it got, passing over the Laramies and into the formidable Rockies.

A dark, indistinguishable shape loomed ahead to the

right. Raider heeled the mare, picking up the pace. His heart quickened. The shape gradually identified itself: the road wagon. It sat at an angle in the rain ditch, Kinsella's gelding still in the shafts, lying on its side lathered and gleaming, run to death. Its flanks were so striped with whip marks, they crisscrossed each other and blended into a single ugly, bloody mess. At first glance it looked like the hide had been peeled from both flanks.

"Heartless son of a bitch! And stupid."

True. For one who usually planned so carefully, thought things through so clearly, Steinbrenner had blundered badly, murdering the animal. If the rear wheel had fallen off, he would have been able to ride the horse. Still, even if that had happened, what with the killing pace he'd set for it, it would have given out in the shafts or out of them.

Raider knelt and examined the horse. Its muzzle was still warm, its whole body. He checked the faulty wheel. It appeared as sound and secure as any of the others. He glanced about, then ahead. Tie Siding was behind them and Redbuttes. Laramie was perhaps ten miles ahead. Was he heading there on foot? Ten miles, lugging those suitcases? Not if he was thinking. Given the fact that he'd never make the 11:58, it made more sense to get off the road with his burden at the first darkened house, catch a night's sleep in the barn, arise bright and early, forgo his morning routine fussing with his mustachios, get back on the road, and hitch a ride to Laramie.

Off he rode, squinting left and right for a sign of ranch buildings. To the left about half a mile distant the moonlight outlined a house, barn, and silo. The forest was well behind Raider. He had climbed deep into cattle country, ranches sprawling over the valleys between the ribs of the mountains.

Steinbrenner was in the barn. Raider sensed it; he knew it. In the warm, comfortable hay already asleep. Ready to be taken.

"Thank you, Lord, for his desperation, cruel streak, and heavy suitcases."

He pulled off into the approach road that led up to the

house, branching before it got there in the direction of the
barn off to one side. He got off the road almost as soon as
he turned into it, dismounting and hobbling the horse. She
tossed her head, swished her tail, and nuzzled him as he
straightened.

"There's a good girl. You stay here outta range. Be back
soon. With him. His luck's run out at last."

Down on one knee, he checked his Peacemaker and,
crouching, started for the barn in a reasonably wide circle,
planning to approach it from the back. All at once, with
discouraging suddenness, the moonlight that had served
him so well up to now turned against him. He hadn't covered ten yards when an upstairs window flew open, the
muzzle of a shotgun poked out, and both barrels thundered.

"Jesus Christ!"

He went into his dive between the two blasts, landing
hard, flattening in the grass.

"Whoever you are down there, I can see you plain as
day. Move a hair and I'll blow your face out the back o'
your head!"

It was a woman's voice.

"Hold your fire. Chrissakes!"

A stoop-shouldered man carrying a Winchester came
bursting out the front door.

"On your feet, fella."

"She just told me—".

"Up!"

The single-shot chewed ground at his feet. He jumped
up like he'd been stung, lifting his hands, dropping his
gun. It was a sensible move, and smart, but unfortunately
not in his best interests. From the first appearance of the
shotgun at the upstairs window to his being ordered to his
feet by the Winchester-wielding man of the house, Raider's
concentration on Steinbrenner understandably deserted
him. The opposite did not hold true. Shots came flying
from inside the barn. The ominous whirring sounds chilled
his spine as the two slugs bracketed him too closely. Down
he went a second time.

"What the hell!" burst the approaching man. "How many of there are you?"

Steinbrenner fired a third shot, a message, for there was no way he could see his target in the tall grass. He followed with a fourth. Panic shooting, decided Raider, coming nowhere near him.

Instead it passed clean through the man's neck. He stopped short, fastened a questioning look upon Raider at his feet, dropped his rifle, and fell dead.

"Howard!" bawled the woman upstairs. "Howard! Are you all right?"

"He's dead!" called Raider, cupping his hand around his mouth.

"Nooooooooooo . . ."

A short pause, a bloodcurdling scream, silence. The breeze picked up, bending the grass. Down came two more blasts from the shotgun, the second one so close he could feel it burn past his cheek.

"Hey, hey, cut it out! I didn't shoot him! Honest! It's him in the barn, the guy I'm after. Please! Don't shoot!"

She held her fire. Steinbrenner did not. He emptied his Gruener, shooting wildly, missing by a wide margin. Funny, thought Raider, how you could tell by a man's shooting how he felt. And Steinbrenner felt panic, desperation. Coolness always spaced shots; fear always hurried them.

"Don't move!" shouted the woman. "I'm coming down."

"Good," muttered Raider disgustedly. This he really needed: hair curlers and skirts coming between them.

His next move leaped to mind: move the battleground as far from Howard's body as he could, around behind the barn. He paused to weigh the situation, what it was at present, what he could make of it. Steinbrenner had cover, he had none, but Steinbrenner was the hub of the wheel. The German had limited movement, while he could approach from whichever side he chose.

He chose the rear. He snaked through the grass, grunting at every sharp stone that came in contact with an

elbow, a rib, his kneecap. He moved widely away from the
house, into a circle around the barn, thinking as he did that
Steinbrenner had to guess what he was up to. And see the
top of the grass moving. He did, firing sporadically until
the moon came to Raider's rescue, sliding behind a cloud,
darkening the landscape.

He could hear the woman sobbing well behind him as
she came up to her husband's body. Steinbrenner was
building up more and more that he'd ultimately have to
account for when he died and appeared at the gates of hell.
At the rate he was killing, he could end up the devil's
right-hand man!

It took Raider fully twenty minutes to get around behind
the barn. In the meantime the moon emerged, shining as
brightly as before. All sides of the barn showed cracks and
knotholes through which Steinbrenner could peer and
shoot. Raider approached a corner. He got within fifteen
yards before the German opened up, sending a flurry at
him, setting him scrambling, crabbing backwards.

"I can see every move you make, my friend!" boomed a
muffled voice. Laughter followed.

Raider did not answer. A little, very small ploy: when
two people shoot at each other from cover and one speaks
and the other does not respond, it invariably makes the
speaker nervous, makes him even more mouthier.

"I will let you come close, just close enough to be certain that I will not miss. Come closer, please, let us get this
over with."

"You got a train to catch, I know," muttered Raider.

At the moment, with no shots coming from the barn and
Raider yet to fire, it looked like a Mexican standoff. Inside, Steinbrenner had limited mobility very much in his
favor. He could move anyplace he pleased—across the
rear, to the sides, back to the front. Raider stiffened, recalling that he had hobbled his horse down near the main
road. Looking in that direction, Steinbrenner couldn't help
but see it. He could ease the barn door softly open and
make a run for it.

"Get away clean. Leave me to shank's mare it after him."

Raider cocked an ear, but all he could hear was the wind. It was blowing away from him, blowing away the sound of the woman's sobbing on the far side. If indeed she still was. He resolved to take no chances. Getting to his feet, crouching low, he sprinted around to the other side and far enough down it to give himself a clear view of the front.

Steinbrenner followed him around with sporadic shooting. Raider wondered how he was doing for ammunition. When he'd stolen the Gruener from Rudy in New York, had his victim been carrying extra cartridges on him? That was doubtful. More likely they would have been in with his luggage. But Steinbrenner had had plenty of opportunity to buy ammunition since then. In Cheyenne? Never. Nobody stocked 9 millimeter, let alone 11. But in Chicago he'd have no trouble getting some. Damn Windy City had everything.

Having flattened in the grass about twenty yards from the side of the barn, using his elbows, Raider pulled himself slowly forward. All was silent inside at the moment, but any second now Steinbrenner would resume shooting. Raider sensed it, his shoulder and neck muscles tightening in expectation. He could almost make out Steinbrenner's eyeball framed by a knothole.

Suddenly the German opened up, emptying his weapon at him, slugs chewing the ground in front of his face, ripping through his hat, creasing his shoulder. The last one found his left shoulder, striking like a hammer, burrowing like a branding iron.

Goddamn it hurt!

He shook off the pain as best he could. Steinbrenner watched him and laughed, a high-pitched, derisive cackling. Raider rolled over, his right hand going to his shoulder, pulling his palm down gloved with blood.

"Damn!"

He stiffened. A door creaked. He was making a break for it. Raider rose to his knees, clenching his teeth fit to

shatter them, summoning his will, driving the pain out of
mind, out of his shoulder. Steinbrenner appeared,
crouched, and broke into a run. Raider two-handed his
gun, aimed, fired, missed. Missed again and again.
Cursed. The pain had set his eyes misting with tears. He
could no longer see clearly. His target was getting farther
and farther away. Out of range. Through the grass to the
hobbled mare.

Suddenly the earth shuddered. The barn seemed to
shake before his eyes as the shotgun blasted. Steinbrenner
stopped short, dropped his weapon, raised his hands. The
woman was starting toward him, the shotgun pointed at his
chest. Raider felt dangerously close to passing out. He
shook and shook his head, trying to rid himself of the
swimming fuzziness.

He staggered to his feet, fought off collapse as his head
whirled, and stumbled forward. He was within ten strides
of them when the woman, standing three lengths of the
shotgun barrel from Steinbrenner, heard him and foolishly
turned to look. Steinbrenner sprang at her, knocking her
flat, the shotgun blowing the second barrel. Down he went,
scrambling, retrieving his gun, crouching behind her, firing
at Raider.

But Raider had lost no time in reacting himself. Prone,
he returned fire, catching the German in the right side. He
roared, dropped his gun and sent his hand to the wound.
And continued bellowing in pain. Raider ran up to him,
kicked the Gruener well out of reach, and suddenly exploded in fury, slamming him in the temple with his gun.

Steinbrenner fell on his side and lay still. Raider picked
up the Gruener and hurled it well away. The woman was
dead, shot in the stomach by her own gun. Steinbrenner
was out cold. Raider holstered his gun and made for the
well. The bucket was up and half-filled. He dashed water
in his face. It helped immeasurably, clearing his head and
his eyes. The slug in his shoulder throbbed mightily. It felt
as if it had caught fire and was trying to burn its way out.
He tore his shirt from it and examined the wound. It didn't

look as deep as it felt. It was hard to tell. Friedland would get it out. Mouthy though he was, he was good.

Leaving the two corpses and the unconscious Steinbrenner, he went into the kitchen. Rummaging through drawers, he found what he was looking for: a pint of what looked like rye. There was no label. He sniffed it. Rye. He downed two healthy swigs and poured two more on his wound. It exploded with pain. "Damn fool! Wha'ja do that for?"

He went back outside and slapped Steinbrenner awake.

"I am dying."

"Oh bullshit, it's just a crease."

"It is deep. Fatal."

"Get up."

"I cannot."

Raider drew his gun. "Try."

Steinbrenner got to his feet grimacing with pain, holding his wound with both hands. "I am bleeding to death."

"I'll give you a couple more holes an' hurry it along if you don't quit with the gripin' an' come along quiet."

"Not back to Cheyenne."

"Back to Cheyenne."

"But that is insane. I will never make it."

"You'll walk to friggin' Chicago if I want you to. Let's get one thing straight out front. I would dearly, I mean dearly love to cash in your chips right here and now, but it's my job to bring you in, so in we go."

"I will never make it."

"You already said. Look at you, for Chrissakes, it's stopped bleedin' already. You hit me in the shoulder before and it still hasn't caked."

He leered viciously. "Perhaps you will bleed to death before we get there."

Raider raised his gun slowly. "Perhaps you will shut up and keep shut up. If, that is, you want to live till the hangman."

FOURTEEN

He slid his warm, welcome hand down her naked thigh, setting it on fire. He kissed her.

"Mmmmm . . ."

The single small lamp on the dressing table sent its pink glow up the wall in an ever-widening vee. Their shadows, blended into one, twisted and writhed slowly. She drew her breath in sharply; his panting became louder and louder still. She groaned in ecstasy and cried out. He smothered her with kisses.

"Three days and already you know everything there is to know about the job," he said admiringly. "You amaze me, my darling."

"I . . . do my best, Anson."

"So I notice."

He stood at the window looking down upon the night-shrouded city, his broad back to her. She came gliding up to him, her dressing gown rustling. She set her hands on his shoulders and pressed her cheek against his back. "I owe it all to you."

He laughed and turned and took her in his arms. "And I'm making you pay in the most valuable currency."

"You're not 'making' me anything. It's all voluntary on my part."

In his arms her thoughts whirled away from him—to the bank, the vault. It had all been so ridiculously easy, so effortless and safe it astounded her. Her new job was to double-check the amounts of the various denominations on hand at the close of business every day, to make certain the individual tellers' figures matched the bank's total. It had been a simple matter to bring her $30,000 to the bank in two packets in the paper sack which looked as if it contained her lunch. Everyone who wasn't an officer brought his lunch in such a manner. Simple, too, to exchange the money for an equivalent amount in genuine twenties. Even now, as he held her, the money reposed in a shoe box under her bed. He was beautiful, she was in love, but Liberty standing with sword and shield, flanked by the lovely white numbers "20" superimposed on black, tooth-edged seals, was even more appealing to her eyes.

"Victoria . . ."

"Mmmmm?"

"I love you."

She melted slightly. He tightened his embrace.

"I love *you,* Anson, my darling." Ask me to marry you, she urged.

"Would you believe you're the first woman I have ever said that to?"

She would be a fool to believe that, she told herself, but it did sound nice.

"Of course I believe you," she lied. "You would never lie to me."

"Not if my life depended on it." He released her and, seizing her hands, held her at arm's length. "You are the most beautiful woman I have ever known, and the brightest. The best in every way."

Then ask me to marry you!

He did not. Instead, he went to the dresser and refilled their glasses from the bottle of champagne. Sitting at the foot of the bed in the most provocative pose she could strike, she watched him. She would give him until the end of the week, until Saturday noon to ask her. If by then he did not, she would ask him.

One way or the other he would be hers. For life. Forever.

Having been wounded himself so many times in so many places by so many different weapons in varying degrees of seriousness, Raider fancied he could judge at a glance the seriousness of others' wounds. He judged Steinbrenner's as a lot less serious than did the victim.

To help him take his mind off it, he put him to work burying the husband and wife. Steinbrenner fumed and complained, bellyaching to the last shovelful tossed on the woman's grave, but he managed to complete the job. Raider then escorted him inside the house, found some long cord in the kitchen, ordered him to bed, and tied him securely.

He then went back outside, freed the horse, brought her into the barn, and fed her bran, oats, and all the hay she could eat. He found Steinbrenner's suitcases and opened them. One was packed with clothes and a half-boxful of cartridges for the Gruener. The other contained paper, a small cutting board, steel plates, bottles of various colored inks and a press broken down into four sections. There was also nearly $20,000 in genuine bills.

He repacked everything and, leaving the suitcases in the barn, returned to the house. Trussed up like a Christmas turkey, "death" wound and all, Steinbrenner still managed to fall asleep. He snored lustily, all but setting the walls vibrating. Raider woke him by ripping his shirt open, sending buttons flying all directions.

"What the devil!"

"Just wanta get the real Rudy's medals, okay? Do you mind? Sorry bout wakin' you."

He ripped them free of Steinbrenner's undershirt and pocketed them.

"What are you starin' at? Go back to sleep. Wait, before

you do, let me tell you somethin'." He tapped the pocket containing the medals. "This here is the absolute lowest of the low in my book. Even shootin' him like you did, him hurtin' an' helpless lyin' on that cot, isn't below stealin' his war medals. Which he earned with his heroism and bravery under fire. For a slacker like you to pin 'em on, that is disgustin'. You're disgustin'!"

"Are you so stupid you do not understand? I assumed his identity, why should I not assume everything that was his? Everything that presented Rudolph Fenstermacher to the world? I did not flaunt them, I merely kept them on me."

"And made believe they were yours, that you fought, you were the hero. As if a bucket o' slime like you ever could be."

"You stupid yokel."

Raider bristled and cuffed him.

"That is it, hit a man when he is tied and helpless."

"Just don't tempt me to kill you while you are. Believe me, it won't take much. Now go back to sleep."

He left the room. Sleep for him inside the house would be impossible, he knew. He repaired to the barn and retired for the night.

They found eggs and a half side of bacon in the cold hole in the kitchen floor. They had breakfast, and afterwards Raider retied the prisoner's hands behind his back. He searched the barn, found rope, fashioned a lariat, and, slipping the noose around Steinbrenner's neck, mounted up and rode back to the main road, trailing him behind. He had tied the handles of the two suitcases together and draped them like saddlebags over the horse's rump.

He marched him back up the road to the wagon in the ditch. The horse's corpse was under siege by legions of flies. He untied Steinbrenner's wrists and put him to work undoing the harness from the dead gelding and preparing the mare for the shafts in its stead. Presently, with Steinbrenner tied hand and foot, knees drawn up so that lying on his side in the little bed behind the seat he fit into it, they set off at a trot for Redbluffs and, four hours ahead, Cheyenne.

Steinbrenner, in spite of his periodic pronouncements to the contrary, appeared all but completely recovered from his "death" wound. He was a tough nut, and luckily the bullet had passed clean through. Raider should only have been so fortunate. At the moment his shoulder was killing him. He was tempted to haul out his gun and blow it away. The slug felt ten times its normal size, burning fiercely and burrowing deeper and deeper into its site. By the time Friedland got it under his knife, he would have to dig clear down to his elbow to get it out.

Apart from hurting like blazes, it did little for his disposition. Without it, he would have felt a sense of triumph, would have been proud and pleased with himself for having wrapped the thing up and collared poor Rudy's killer. With his wound, he couldn't care less, and opted to plunge into the black doldrums and flounder about.

He didn't speak to Steinbrenner, but Steinbrenner never stopped talking to him. Halfway between Borie and Cheyenne, the German played his only card—his ace.

"How much do they pay you, Raider? Enough? Fairly for risking your life. For your shoulder? For all your wounds? All the close calls? You looked inside my suitcases, I am sure. You saw the money. There is nearly twenty thousand. It is all yours, and there is more where that came from."

Raider responded for the first time. "You figgerin' on printin' up another lot?"

"That money is genuine."

"Mmmmm."

"Look at it closely, you'll see. Take it, my friend, every penny, untie me, and look the other way."

"Sure."

"You agree?"

"Sure. The agency pays me nickels and dimes; headaches, sufferin', an' ungratefulness by the barrelful. Twenty friggin' thousand would set me up for life."

"Absolutely. Let me go, you'll never hear from me again. I'll . . . I'll get out of the country. I'll go back to—"

"You promise!"

"On my sacred word of honor as a gentleman. Stop the horse! Untie me!"

Raider pulled up and turned in his seat. The sun was approaching its zenith. He removed his Stetson and poked a finger through the 11-millimeter-sized hole. He gazed down at Steinbrenner.

"Untie me!"

"No need. I can getcha outta the mess you're in lots easier."

So saying, he drew his gun and set the muzzle against Steinbrenner's forehead. Steinbrenner gasped. Before Raider's eyes the color drained from his face, leaving it as white as the paper in his suitcase.

"You wouldn't," he rasped.

"Lemme put it this way—I've brought in scum by the bucket: women killers, child killers, men so rotten to the core they've killed their own folks, brothers an' sisters. I've brought in torturers, them that's swindled widows an' orphans, what you'd call the drags of society. But you, Gerhard, are the prize. The worst I ever saw. You no more deserve to live than a rattler."

He cocked the gun.

"No!"

Raider held his hand steady as stone, scowling fiercely. Then he sighed and slowly reholstered his gun.

"One more peep and I won't say nothin', I'll just draw an' fire. Try me, please."

To Victoria von Werder's annoyance and disappointment, Anson Sterling, although coming tantalizingly close on several occasion, failed to fall over the edge into her heart and ask for her hand. She was working in the vault one afternoon, counting and recounting stacks and stacks of money just before closing time. Touching so much money, hundreds of thousands of dollars, surrounded by it, immersed in it, gave her a giddy feeling. But everything good that had happened to her over the past few days could not erase a small worry at the back of her mind.

She had already made the switch, already had $30,000 in authentic twenty-dollar bills safely tucked away. She could leave town anytime and with such a sum flee to anywhere in the world. But she had fallen in love and could not desert the object of her adoration. Gerhard Steinbrenner had been completely eclipsed by Anson. In less than a week he had become her sun, the stars, the universe. She was crazy about him. And he, she was certain, felt the same way about her. He certainly talked as if he did. He was unsparing in his flattery, in voicing his devotion. There could be no doubt whatsoever but that he loved her deeply.

If he failed to pop the question, she would do it for him. By Saturday noon. She'd propose, he'd accept. Then what? She would have to tell him about the switch; tell him that in the vault, destined to be slowly passed out to the unsuspecting public by the equally unsuspecting tellers until it was all in circulation, was $30,000 in bogus tens.

She would have to tell him. She had wracked her brain and could see no way to keep it from him. To be sure, that didn't mean there *was* no way. There had to be. She simply hadn't hit on it yet.

She supposed she could mail the money home to her mother in Germany to hold for her until she got there. But when she married Anson he might not want to drop his job and run off to Germany. She'd be surprised if he agreed to. However she looked at it, the damned money was a problem.

Standing thinking about it, she failed to notice him come into the vault and sneak up behind her. When he kissed her on the neck she jumped a foot. He apologized and helped her pick up the money she'd dropped.

"I want to go back to the hotel to bed," he whispered.

"Shame on you!"

"You don't?"

"I do, I do."

"We close in six minutes. Can you wait six minutes? I don't know if I can."

"The bank closes, but it'll be until five o'clock before I finish totaling for the day."

"Let it go."

"I can't. Please, don't tempt me."

"I'll take the responsibility. Come in early tomorrow morning."

"Can I?"

"Of course. Come in an hour early." He pecked her on the cheek and backed away. At the door he paused. "Six minutes. Five and thirty seconds."

They sat naked opposite each other on the bed. He handed her a glass of champagne. "To us, my darling. Now and forever."

This is it, she told herself, it will be now. A sip, an endearing glance, a smile, then: "Will you marry me?"

They sipped. He smiled, leaned over, and kissed her. Then he finished his glass, got up, and started to dress.

"Where are you going?" she asked, doing her utmost to conceal her surprised disappointment.

"Business, love."

"At this time of night?"

"It's only eight-thirty."

"But what . . ."

"For Mr. Hoffler."

The president of the bank. The mention of his name conjured up a vision of his shining pate, pinch glasses, walrus mustaches, and voice that sounded as if it were coming up from the bottom of a dry well.

"You're coming back?"

"I'm afraid it'll be quite late, too late. Besides, you have to be at the bank early tomorrow."

"I need my beauty sleep."

"My darling, I'm sure you could stay up all night and it wouldn't tire your beauty. You are *so* beautiful."

Again he kissed her. Two minutes later he was gone.

Tomorrow was Friday, she thought as she closed the door. Perhaps Friday evening he would pop the question. It was no longer a question of if, only when. And he would.

She would not have to ask him after all. The mere thought of doing so repelled her. It wasn't, as some women thought, the assertiveness of a free and independent spirit; it was demeaning, it was a plea. Nevertheless, she would not hesitate if by Saturday noon he failed to ask her.

"He will."

She arrived at the bank an hour early and was let in by the janitor. She easily completed the work left from the previous day before the bank opened at eight. Anson did not appear. By ten in the morning he still hadn't shown up. Nor did he by noontime. Mr. Hoffler came to her desk shortly after twelve. The fact that she and Anson were interested in one another was no secret.

"Any idea where he might be, Miss von Werder?" Hoffler quietly boomed, his voice rising from low in his generous paunch. "It's not like him not to show up for work. I can't remember the last time he was out. Never ill, never absent, always on time. To be honest, I'm getting worried."

His admission increased her own concern.

"I can't imagine where he is. We had dinner last night. That was the last I saw of him."

"He didn't say anything?"

"Nothing about staying out today."

"I've already sent the boy around to his apartment. Nobody home. I sure hope nothing's happened. Cross your fingers he shows up after lunch."

He did not. The day ended with no sign of him. She rushed to finish her work and went straight to Howard Street. She knocked and knocked, but there was no response. None to her call.

She scribbled a note, telling him she was worried, everyone at the bank was, and would he please come to the hotel—if he couldn't, send word that he was all right. She went back to the hotel and ordered a drink from room service, hoping it would settle her nerves. It failed to. To fill the time, to take her mind off her worries about him, she got out the $30,000 and counted it.

At seven she went out for dinner. On the way to the

restaurant she stopped by his apartment. The corner of her note was still visible, peeking from under the door.

By now she was beside herself. It was so unlike him, she was certain he had met with some sort of accident. This conclusion arrived at, the accident became terrible, fatal. Should she go to the police? See if they knew anything? She should but was afraid to, afraid they *would* know and her worst fears would be realized.

She walked past Reutter's Restaurant on Fifth Street. It had a reputation for excellent food and a delightful atmosphere. It was expensive, but she could afford it; besides, she felt she deserved to pamper herself after such a dreadful day and evening. Surrounded by the subtly classic and utterly charming decor of vine-covered wrought iron, sparkling chandeliers, monogrammed linen, and gleaming crystal, she was escorted to a table for one in a private little corner. To her left as she took her chair two large columns rose, between them a lush potted plant, completely concealing the line of tables against the wall on the other side.

She ordered a glass of white wine and, given the menu, decided on foie de veau Grande Bretagne. It proved superb, absolutely delicious. She had barely tasted it when the sound of voices broke through the interminable clinking of silverware and crystal and indistinguishable conversation of the other diners within view.

"You are the most beautiful woman I have ever known. And the brightest, the best in every way."

She sat bolt upright. The words were familiar; she recognized the voice.

"So you have said, many times. Darling, you do say the most beautiful things."

"To the loveliest woman I know, have ever known, and the most deserving of compliments. I've missed you so these two weeks."

"Only eleven days."

"It seemed like years."

"And were you a good boy? Did you spend every night alone in your room, counting the hours until my return?"

"You're not suggesting I'd see another woman behind your back!"

"I'm not suggesting anything."

"You really don't know me very well, do you?"

"Don't pout. You look like a little boy. Anson, you're handsome, debonair, an eyeful, and a catch for any woman. Temptation must be thrown in your path every day."

"Hardly, my dear, but when it is I know how to resist it. You're much too precious to risk losing."

"Is everything set for tomorrow morning?"

"Of course. I've had nothing but time on my hands since you left."

"You have the money?"

"Two hundred thousand."

"And arranged our passage?"

"We sail at the crack of dawn."

"Oh no! I'll have to get up at midnight to be ready and down at the dock. How could you, darling?"

"Calm yourself, I said we *sail* at dawn. We board at midnight."

"Oooooo . . . Wonderful. We'll go right to bed, of course."

"May I take that as an invitation? And when we awaken tomorrow morning, we'll be miles out to sea. Are you finished? Let's get out of here. We'll go back to your place. I'll help you pack."

"Is that *all* you want to do?"

He laughed lightly; she echoed him. The stunned and silent eavesdropper heard fingers snap. The waiter came scurrying over.

"Check, please."

Moments later they got up and left. She shrank into the corner nearest the column to keep from being seen. His companion was tall, blond, and beautiful. She was expensively dressed in a full-length gown of blue silk, and her shoulders were hung with foxes. They did not look back. They passed out of sight into the foyer. She pictured them saying their good-nights to the people out front and going out into the street.

She felt as if she had been struck from behind. Her lungs seemed to constrict; breathing was difficult. She sat so stiffly, so firmly clamped in shock, she feared every bone would shatter. She was perspiring; nausea struck in the pit of her stomach and began to spread. Her throat felt so dry she was afraid to swallow, afraid she might crack her windpipe.

The waiter came over. He bowed stiffly and put on his oiliest, most obviously ingratiating grin. "Is everything all right, Miss?"

FIFTEEN

"I'll say this," said Friedland, straightening up after examining Raider's shoulder. "He got off one helluva lot easier than you. A quarter inch to the right your bullet would have missed him completely. As it is it passed in and out slick as a greased needle."

"The sonovabitch!" boomed Raider. "Goddamn faker! We pulled into town, he passed out cold. Faked it, he did. I had to carry him inside the damn jail. You saw, Mace. And me with this killin' me. He even kept playin' possum all the while I was goin' through his pockets."

"It's possible he wasn't faking," said Friedland. "He did lose a lot of blood. He was white as a sheet."

"I wish he was wrapped in one!"

"Find anything in his pockets?" Tunstall asked.

"Buncha little notebooks. Musta been six or seven. I flipped through 'em. I was so close to passin' out myself I was damned if I'd stay there and let him see me. Over on the table there are Rudy's medals and papers. It's all gotta be sent back to Germany to his boss. Owwww."

"Hurt?" Friedland leered.

"Funny man."

"If it doesn't hurt now I can guarantee it will. That bullet's in there about a foot."

"Can you get it out and save my arm?"

"I'll do my best." He clapped a hand against Raider's forehead. "You're running about a hundred and ten fever. Lie down before you fall down."

The powerful stench of alcohol mingling with other odors pervaded the little examining room. Raider lay flat. He was sweating furiously. The doctor patted the sweat from his face. "Try and relax."

"Sure. While you hack me to pieces like so much stew beef. Mace . . ."

"What?"

"You got Jethro or somebody keepin' a eye on his nibs? Keepin' a eye on his little door openin'?"

"No. He's not going anywhere."

"He's slick as a bayou eel. His neck's really on the line now. He'll try to get away."

"How can he?"

"Mmmmm."

"Do you always worry so much about everything?" Friedland asked.

"Did you send that telegram to Chicago like I asked?"

Tunstall nodded. "Addressed directly to Chief Pinkerton. Informing him of Fenstermacher's death, Steinbrenner's capture."

"My near fatal wound?"

"That, too, and that you'll be bringing him in as soon as you're back on your feet."

"Good boy."

"Ready when you are," said Friedland. "Want to watch this, Mace, or do you have something else to do?"

"I've no shortage of 'to do,' thank you. I'll drop by later, Raider. Good luck."

"Whatta you mean 'good luck'!" He scowled at Friedland. "What does he mean? Is this dangerous? Can you handle it? You ever take a bullet out from this deep before? Have you? Have you!"

"Dozens, hundreds. I lost count twenty years ago. Look here, do you know what these are?"

"Bill forceps."

Friedland was impressed. "Very good. How'd you know?"

"Invented by U.S. Army surgeon J. H. Bill. Hundred years ago my then partner, Weatherbee, took a arrowhead outta my rear end with 'em. You know how to use 'em?"

"No, but with a little practice . . . Of course I know!"

Tunstall left. Raider groaned him out the door.

"I'm going to give you chloroform. You won't feel a thing. When you wake up the slug'll be sitting on your chest and you'll feel fit as a fiddle."

"I'll bet."

"In a week, give or take ten days. Seriously, I see no insurmountable problems. Your shoulder will be stiff, probably for the rest of your days, but that's not the only part, I'm sure. You must have two dozen old wounds in your chest and back alone. That hole under your heart must have been six times as bad as this."

"I'll still keep my arm?"

"I don't want it."

"I mean I'll be able to use it like before. Proper."

"You will."

The cone dropped over Raider's nose and mouth. Down splashed a few drops of chloroform.

"Breathe deeply and count backwards from one hundred."

"I can't count backwards, damn it! Who the hell counts backwards? What's the use?"

"My God, forward then."

He got to eleven, pushed out twelve, and slipped under. Friedland examined the wound under his magnifying glass.

"Good God what a hole. You're something else, Pinkerton. Any ordinary man would have passed out and stayed out. Well, Doctor, let's get to digging."

* * *

The sickly sweet taste of the chloroform disguised the dryness in his mouth at first. Eyelids still tightly sealed, the stink of carbolic acid struck his nostrils. His brain only vaguely aware that it was freeing itself from unconciousness, he put his tongue to work exploring his mouth. From the effort it took to move it, he imagined his mouth was stuffed with cotton. He groaned, raised his head from the pillow, glanced left, and dropped his head down. His shoulder was neatly wrapped in an ascending spica. The smell of carbolic was coming from there. He could see his shoulder rounding the dressing, but could not feel it. He felt nothing in that area, as if his shoulder all the way across his neck and down his arm had been lopped off.

There was no pain, but he did not dare test it, deciding that if he tried it would explode with agony so intense he would black out. He was alone in the room. He could hear bottles clicking in the other room, the sound of pouring, and a low, toneless whistling. Presently Friedland came out. His smock was stained with blood. His, Raider thought. He should draw his attention to it; he'd maybe deduct something from the bill. Probably not.

"Welcome back."

"How'd it go?"

"It was deep. I nearly hit your wrist."

"Seriously."

Friedland fished the slug from his pocket and held it up for his appraisal. "Want it?"

"Hell no. Chrissakes, if I kept every slug dug outta me in my side pocket, I'd friggin' walk with a limp. Can I get up?"

"Not yet. Try and sleep."

"I been."

"Natural sleep. Best medicine right now."

"What time is it?"

"About eight, eight-thirty. Why? Going somewhere?"

"I feel weak as a fish."

"Hungry?"

"Starved."

"I'll get you something hot and decent."

"Maybe a snort o' somethin', too?"

"I'll try. You go to sleep. When you wake up, you can eat like a horse. Any pain? Don't . . . Don't even think of trying to move it. It's got eleven stitches. It's tender as hell. Give it a day or so."

"Flat on my back?"

"Maybe by tomorrow sitting up. I'll have to strap your arm to your chest. There can't be any movement. Absolutely none. Go to sleep."

She tossed and turned and seethed all night long. And hated him, even more intensely than Steinbrenner. Viciously! Hated all men. Hated small boys who would grow up to become men. Old men because they had fathered boys that grew up. Hated them with a passion! Hated blonds, too. Blonds with foxes. Blonds without.

If only one or the other had divulged the name of their ship. At three in the morning she decided to get up, get dressed, and go down to the docks. Walk up and down, write down the name of every vessel of size; later in the day she would check with the harbormaster. Once she was able to pin down their ship it would be a simple matter to determine its destination across the water. Then what? Alert the Japanese police or Chinese or Malayan and have them both arrested?

On what charge? Jilting her?

There was a better one, much better. She had overheard him mention $200,000. And it did sound like he had embezzled it. He'd lowered his voice when he said the amount. But if he hadn't stolen it, if it was rightfully his . . .

She went back to bed and slept fitfully a couple of hours before getting up for the day. By the time she showed up for work she looked like the wrath of God in the bank window. She felt wretched; on top of a heart so broken, so utterly demolished, it would never mend.

"Men!"

She wasn't at work two minutes when Mr. Hoffler approached her. He looked as bad as she felt.

"Would you please come into my office, Miss von Werder?" he asked quietly.

He gestured her to lead the way. He set his visitor's chair for her, closed the door, and sat behind his desk.

"Any news of Anson?"

"Nothing," she lied, reasoning that the destruction of her life and her broken heart were none of his business.

"I thought not. I'm afraid I have some distressing news."

He reached into the drawer snugged against his watch chain and brought out an envelope. Out of it he produced a twenty-dollar bill identical to the twenties reposing in the shoe box under her bed.

"Please examine it."

She did so. He sat, watched silently, curling the ends of his mustache as he waited. She glanced up at him.

"See anything wrong with it?"

"I . . ."

"It's counterfeit." She gasped. "Somebody planted two hundred thousand dollars' worth in the vault. An employee, obviously. Who else would have free access, eh? Anson's gone, and so is the money. Putting two and two together . . ."

"Good God!" she blurted.

He'd swindled the bank. He'd swindled her!

"My reaction precisely. My very words when I discovered it."

"An . . . An . . . An . . ."

"I beg your pardon?"

"An . . . An . . ."

"Ah, Anson. I do hate to speak ill of the absent, but his disappearance, not a whisper from him, now the money . . ."

At this point she could have told him about the conversation she had overheard at Reutter's. He would have understood why she had hesitated to tell him earlier, it being so personal, not to mention that it made her look embarrassingly foolish, the classic cast-aside victim of an abandoned flirtation. That's all it was to him, the philandering pig! Liar! Swine!

"I treated him like a son," he went on. "It hurts." He looked appropriately pained. "The nerve of the fellow. Two hundred thousand. I do seem to be a terrible judge of character. He's the last person I would have . . . oh, well. I've alerted the police, whatever good it'll do. He's fled by ship, of course. When you steal anything in a port city, that's the fastest, really the only way to get out. He could be in Australia in a week. My dear Miss von Werder, forgive me for rattling on so. Dear me, you look frightfully distressed! May I get you a glass of water?"

"No thank you."

"Brandy?"

"No, I'm all right. Really."

"You don't look it. Perhaps this will cheer you up. On top of the bad, I have some good news. For you personally. First, allow me to congratulate you on the excellent job you're doing for us. Brace yourself. Starting this coming Monday, your salary will be raised from the current eight dollars a week to ten dollars."

He rose and offered his hand.

"Congratulations! Keep up the good work."

SIXTEEN

"You sure you don't want this?" Friedland asked, scratching his beard with one hand and tossing and catching the 11-millimeter slug gouged from Raider's shoulder. "Souvenir?"

"I already tolja I don't. But wait, don't throw it away. Give it to Tunstall to compare with the one you dug outta Rudy's corpse. They'll match like twin brothers. Make good evidence in court against Steinbrenner."

Raider was sitting up in a chair. He had just finished a bowl of pea soup. It was hot, delicious, and bracing. He felt good. His shoulder felt stiff as stone, but the rest of him was swiftly rebounding from the surgery. A mild dizziness whirled his head when he moved about the room, but Friedland assured him it was only temporary.

The doctor excused himself and went into the other room. Tunstall came in. Raider took one look, started, groaned, and threw up his one free hand.

"He escaped!"

"Now don't get excited."

"What the hell you mean, don't get . . . How? You left

151

the cell door unlocked! One of your misfit deputies did. You . . ."

"Will you shut up and let me explain?"

"What's to explain? What the hell good is an alibi?"

"Nobody left his door open! Even if, one chance in ten million, one of us did, the front door was locked. He went out the window. Last night. It must have taken him four hours to saw through the bars."

"Saw?"

Friedland reappeared holding his opened satchel in one hand. He glanced about the room, searching.

"Strange. My amputation saw is missing. Last I knew it was in with everything else. I didn't take it out. Didn't touch it. I haven't sawed bone in two months."

"You sonovabitch!" rasped Raider.

The accusation, so sudden and so vitriolic, startled Friedland. He backed away.

"Shut up!" boomed Tunstall. "Sit still, goddamn it." He looked toward Friedland. "You treated Steinbrenner. When you weren't looking—"

"He filched your saw outta your bag!" exclaimed Raider. "Shoved it under his pillow, and last night sawed through the bars and escaped. Thanks a lot, Doc. Jesus Christ! I catch 'em, you treat 'em and help 'em get away."

"Now just a damn minute!" A sudden flush of bravado did not completely hide Friedland's guilty expression and tone. "I may have turned my back . . . I . . ."

Raider bristled. 'Whatta you mean, 'may'? Why didn't you reach in the damn bag and hand him the damn thing? You might as well have."

"I never dreamed . . . All right! I was careless; he took advantage."

"Leave him alone, Raider, what's done is done. I'm sorry."

"Good. That makes everything okay." He sighed. "It's not *your* fault, except if you'd have put a deputy on his door hole like I asked you to, he wouldn't have been able to saw nothin'. Man oh man oh man, if this don't beat all."

"I haven't checked yet," said Tunstall, "but he probably

stole the first horse he came across and is heading back to Laramie. How badly was he wounded, Doc?"

"Not bad enough to slow him down. Not as bad as this one. It's easy to see which is the better shot."

Raider ignored the barb. "Wherever he's headin', it's only the first stop. He'll likely catch the train in Laramie and head for San Francisco."

The sheriff looked puzzled. "How do you know that?"

"I tolja I went through his pockets, his notebooks. The back page in one had a whole list of cities. Cheyenne was next-to-last. Last was Frisco."

"But see here, he knows you went through his notebooks; you did say he was awake."

"I dunno if he was or wasn't. Playin' possum or not."

Tunstall shook his head disconsolately. "I don't know, Raider. It seems to me . . . I mean if *I* passed out and was carrying that sort of information, I'd sure know you'd be going through my pockets and find it. How could you not? In which case, San Francisco would be the last place *I'd* go."

"Maybe, maybe not. He could take a chance. He's got a head start. Even if he only beats me there by an hour or so, that's time enough to do what he's got to and get out."

Friedland stared. "And what might that be?"

"Hook up with his accomplice, the woman. The one Fish's teller went gaga over and she used and he blew his brains out. Every place her and Steinbrenner bilk, she gets there first. She plants the counterfeit, collects the genuine money; he gets there like a week after. Unless I'm dead wrong, she's in Frisco this very moment doin' what she does so well to some poor slob in some bank. She'll likely have the whole scam wrapped up by the time Steinbrenner gets there. Yes sir, that's where they'll rendezvous, that's where I'll catch 'em both!

"I gotta make fast tracks. Once he connects with her they won't hang around. They'll get out like always. And if they do, Chrissakes I'll never catch 'em."

Tunstall nodded. "What you say does make sense."

"Course."

"I see only one fly in your ointment," said Friedland airily.

"Don't pay no attention to him, Mace, there's no flies."

"One. You, my friend, are not going anywhere. You wouldn't get as far as Laramie before you collapse. I shouldn't have to remind you that you have just undergone a very nearly major operation. That's how deep I went in. You've got a hole there you could hide your index finger in. Oh, you may think you can ride a horse and travel and handle yourself like you did when you were a hundred percent, but your body will tell you otherwise. You are going nowhere for at least one week."

"Right."

"He didn't hear a word." Friedland looked appealingly at the sheriff.

Tunstall grinned. "Keep talking, Doc, maybe you'll eventually get through."

Raider got up slowly. He stood reeling slightly, shook off the dizziness, widened his eyes, and blinked rapidly. Then he took a cavernous breath and let it out slowly.

"I'm A-one. I feel strong as a horse. I'll recuperate on the train. By the time I get to Frisco I'll be aces."

"I forbid you to leave!"

"You don't happen to know when the next train is?" Raider asked Tunstall.

"Forbid, do you hear? If you'd had the presence of mind of a two-year-old when you searched him, you would have taken his money. That would certainly have slowed him down." Friedland leered.

"And if you'd had the presence of mind of a fifty-year-old, you'da locked your damn bag and stuck it well outta his reach when you worked on him. If you had done that, I wouldn't be havin' to do this, damn it!"

Either through an oversight or because, in light of Steinbrenner's escape with his amputation saw, Friedland's conscience forbade him, he neglected to bill Raider for his services. Not to be outdone, Raider conveniently neglected to ask how much he owed him.

Behind the patient's back Friedland appealed to Tunstall to at least try to talk him out of picking up the pursuit. The sheriff tried. Raider had no ears for either man. By the time he got his clothes on one-handed and got over to the office with Tunstall, the sheriff had to help him through the door to his chair.

"It's just my knees," explained Raider. "Not usin' 'em for a whole day always makes 'em wobbly."

"Sure. You sure you want to take off right away?"

"You already asked that fifteen times. Just lay off. I know what I'm doin'. Besides, if I don't get after him soon he'll get to Frisco and be halfway to China by the time I don't catch up with him."

"What? Never mind. Got enough money?"

"I never got enough, but I'm okay."

"I know you travel free on your pass, but you really ought to spring for a berth, so you can at least get a decent night's sleep."

"U.P. berth is two bucks extra a night. Three nights, maybe four . . . Eight bucks is a friggin' fortune. The chief doesn' reimburse for luxuries like sleepin' berths or meals on the train 'steada off at the station. And maybe it'll turn out I'll need that eight bucks for shells and such.

"I been thinkin', Mace, I could have a real good edge on him. He doesn't know the railroad like I do. The other side of the Green River, the train stops at Bryan, then Granger. At Granger, folks headin' direct to Frisco got to change over to the Southern Pacific. If he *is* headin' for there and doesn't change over, he'll end up in Portland, Oregon, and have to take the S.P. spur down to Davis to pick up the Central Pacific for the run into Frisco. That takes a lot more time than straight across the southern route."

"Doesn't the conductor remind the passengers that they have a choice before Granger?"

"Comin' outta Omaha at the start of the run the ticket people give 'em their choice of the scenic route or the more direct. The thing is, all the way to the Coast, Granger is the only stop where you can change over. First and last."

"If that's the case, the conductor would have to announce it."

"He likely does, only his nibs might not be payin' attention. He might be snoozin', might miss hearin' it for one reason or some other." Raider nodded, agreeing wholeheartedly with himself.

"I think you're being overly optimistic on that one."

"It's still a possibility. What time you got?"

"Eleven oh eight." He got out the train schedule. "You've only got twenty minutes. Got everything?"

"Another thing, if he did head for Laramie like before, I can pick up about three hours on him right there."

"It won't do you much good if he left before midnight or shortly after. That would put you a good five or six hours behind." The sheriff nodded.

"Thatta boy, look at the bright side."

"Come on, I'll help you over to the station."

"I don't need help!"

"I mean walk with you. I'll miss you, Raider. You're one of a kind. Friedland will too, I'm sure. Boy, you sure left him hot under the collar."

"It'll cool. Don't forget to give him back his saw. "He's a good man, but he just doesn't understand the whacha'callit, ur . . . ur . . ."

"Urgency."

"Right. This is life or death, Mace. Good as. I don't catch up with 'em out there, I could be chasin' the next ten years."

"I'll send another wire to Chicago for you. Tell them there's been a slight hitch."

"Don't do that. Ol' A.P.'ll think it's my fault. He always does. He wouldn't give me the benefit of the doubt if I gave him ten bucks first." In four or five days I'll wire him from out there, when I can tell him it's all wrapped up. Again."

"Good luck, let me know how you make out."

"If you don't hear, you'll know I didn't. Hey . . ."

"What now?"

"I clean forgot the twenty thousand in his suitcase. Genuine, legit."

The suitcases stood side by side near the potbelly stove.

"I can borrow a couple hundred. I . . ."

"Again what?''

"I'm forgettin', that's the Cattleman's Bank's money. Return it to Fish, okay?"

"Will do. Let's go."

SEVENTEEN

Victoria von Werder sat in her suite in the Crocker House tearing up the $30,000 in counterfeit twenty-dollar bills one by one. At the rate she was tearing it would take her a very long time, but she did not mind dragging it out; actually, it was deliberate. With every rip she imagined she was not tearing paper but human skin: that of a certain absent vice-president. And imagined that he screamed in agony each time.

She paused in her torturing to look about her luxurious surroundings. She snickered, then broke into laughter, a wall-ringing, thoroughly unladylike, raucous guffaw. She caught herself and lowered her voice and twisted the ends of an invisible walrus mustache in imitation of Mr. Hoffler.

"This coming Monday your current salary of eight dollars a week will be raised to ten. Congratulations, keep up the good work."

Again she roared. Then sobered. She could ill afford these sumptuous quarters on such a paltry sum. Twenty dollars a week on ten dollars' salary? She sighed. Like it or not—and the very thought chilled her spine—it was to be back to square one. To Steinbrenner. Pick up where she

159

had left off. No problem as far as he was concerned. He
had no idea she'd planned to quit him.

"Oh dear..."

She stiffened. "What will he say when I tell him I exchanged our phony thirty thousand for thirty in phony
twenties? That aren't even as good quality as his? Oh
dear..."

She thought about it. She could leave town before he
got there. With what? The expense money he'd given her
was now reduced by more than half. How far could she get
on what remained and pay for food and lodgings? Not even
back to New York, much less aboard ship and across the
Atlantic.

It was Sunday. He should be arriving today or tomorrow
at the latest. She could see no choice but to get dressed, go
downstairs to the desk, and tell them she was expecting
him; describe him; tell them that he'd be asking for Fräulein Hauser. They'd wonder why she'd registered under a
different name, but there'd be no need to explain. She'd
pay her bill for the week to allay any suspicion they might
have that she was out to cheat them.

She counted her money, adding her salary less one day,
having started at the bank on Tuesday. Deducting the price
of the suite, the total came to $177. Where had it all gone?
She'd spent over $200 since Cheyenne.

She put her money away, restored the shoe box to her
lap, and picked up one of Anson's twenty-dollar bills. She
was about to resume her tearing when she paused to examine it. It definitely wasn't as good quality as Steinbrenner's; still, it *had* passed and evidently for some time. It
had fooled her! Perhaps she should hang on to the rest;
there was still more than $20,000 intact.

Should she attempt to pass one in payment for her hotel
bill? Too risky. An idea flashed. Why not simply hand the
box to Steinbrenner? He'd hardly check to see if the money
was counterfeit. He'd have no earthly reason to suspect.
He'd just take the lion's share, as he usually did, and pro-
ceed to spend it.

That he couldn't do any more than she could risk paying

her bill with one. Hoffler had to have the word out that it had been dumped on the bank and much if not most of it already distributed. He would have to own up to preserve his and the bank's reputation; the discovery couldn't possibly come from someone else.

What a mess. She would have to tell Steinbrenner. She could see no way around it. The short of it was that she had exchanged $30,000 in perfectly good, eminently passable tens for $30,000 in poorly counterfeited twenties.

He'd go wild! Rant and rave. But being yelled at for stupidity and carelessness would be far preferable to his wrath if he suspected she was trying to cheat him.

"What a life. Damn your larcenous soul, Anson Sterling! May your ship sink, may the two of you drown screaming, may your souls rot in hell!"

She sat unmoving with the box in her lap picturing Steinbrenner's arrival. Wishing for it, and soon. When she told him the bad news and he lit into her, after a time he would tire of listening to himself, of repeating the same accusations, condemnation, sarcasm, and insults, and they would sit down and work out a plan of some sort.

Yes, by all means she had to stay and wait for him. For economic reasons if nothing else. She was practically broke; he was bringing nearly $20,000.

Gerhard Steinbrenner's train arrived, depositing him on the ramp in Union Station. Moments later he came out of the same door she had come out of the week before. To be greeted by the same bright sunlight and a similar sight of milling crowds.

He paused before approaching a cab at the curb. He withdrew into the shadows, got out his money, and counted it. And groaned. Damn that yokel, that saddle tramp, he thought. Damn him to death! He'd had him in his sights. He should have blown his head off.

"Thirty-two twenty."

Twenty thousand down the drain. Press, plates, inks, stock, everything gone.

"Thirty-two twenty."

Oh well, no use crying over spilt milk. He should look at the bright side: he did get away, got here, and she was waiting at the hotel.

"With thirty thousand."

"Nineteen thousand five hundred and forty-two. I've counted it three times."

"That's what *I* got,' said Tunstall.

D. O. Fish's brow furrowed, and he assumed an expression of disappointment. "Where's the rest?"

"I'm afraid that's it."

"Did *you* recover it?" Fish's eyes narrowed suspiciously.

"The Pinkerton," Said Tunstall.

"And got his sticky fingers into it and took a recovery fee, is that it?"

"It is not. If it's short, blame the counterfeiter and his accomplice."

"Four hundred and fifty-eight short. It's disappointing, Mason."

"I should think you'd be overjoyed. Raider was badly wounded in recovering it. So it's not every penny, it's damn close. What the hell do you expect, the full amount plus two percent interest?"

"No need to get huffy." Fish lowered his head and peered out from under his upper lids. "Is what I heard true? The prisoner broke out of your jail? That's a fine kettle of fish."

"I don't know why it should worry you. You got your money back."

"Most of it. Ahem, thanks to you."

"I wish I could say you're welcome. I have to go. I have to return a saw."

Raider watched the little depot of Belmont slide away. It sat at the base of gently rolling, treeless hills. In a few minutes they'd be pulling into Union Station. He was wrung out, he felt as if every bone in his body had been removed, and his shoulder bothered him. But none of these things troubled him as much as the realization of what he would be up against upon arriving in San Francisco. All he had to go on was the fact that Steinbrenner was heading there; he had no idea which hotel he'd be checking into or even if he planned to stay in one. Wherever he landed, he wouldn't be staying long.

"This is gonna be some tough row to hoe."

If he never did catch up with him, if the two of them boarded a ship and sailed away to South America, he'd at least succeeded in cutting a healthy chunk out of Mr. Mustache's pride: getting Fish's money back, getting Steinbrenner's press and plates and the rest, putting an end to his efforts in the U.S. Not a bad score, though not nearly as good as collaring him.

He thought about Fenstermacher. To feel sorry for someone he'd never known, never even spoken to, seemed to be stretching it, but piecing together the detective's experiences since New York City, his suffering at Steinbrenner's hands, his failures, his difficulties, his brutal murder, inspired strong feelings of genuine sympathy.

As for himself, he saw that what he needed now was a break: plain, old-fashioned luck. He put himself in Steinbrenner's place. As soon as he got in he'd contact the woman.

"Damn, I don't even know her name!"

Not that either of them would be using their real names here. When they did hook up, what then? She would already have planted the counterfeit and collected the genuine. There'd be no reason for them to hang around. Steinbrenner had to know he was on his tail. He'd want to get out as soon as he could make arrangements.

He laid the flat of his hand gently against his shoulder. It throbbed dully, but not nearly as painfully as it might have from such a deep wound. Still, he'd be one-arming it for a while. Thank God his shooting hand wasn't at the other end.

The second thing Steinbrenner would do upon arrival would be to buy a gun to replace the Gruener, if he hadn't already done so at some stop en route. Maybe they'd both be armed.

The conductor appeared at the end of the car. "Last stop, San Francisco. Please look to your belongings. Thank you for traveling the Union Pacific. Last stop . . ."

He needed a plan, a gem: something that would save him precious time tracking down Steinbrenner. He had neither time nor the stamina to drag it out. There had to be forty or fifty hotels in town. Near the wharf alone were the Illinois House, the Broadway House, Broadway Hotel, Lovejoy's, the Lafayette. Market Street had its share: Lucky Baldwin's two-million-dollar House of Gold, the Palace. Steinbrenner probably hadn't set his accomplice up in any of Nob Hill's hostelries: the St. Francis, the Fairmont, the Mark Hopkins. Too out of the way. Forty or fifty, maybe sixty.

He sat thinking, ignoring the train's stopping, the bustling and activity as the other passengers got off. In moments he found himself alone in the car. The conductor reappeared at the end, eyeing him questioningly.

"I'm comin', I'm comin'."

He was the last one up the ramp into the station, but his lollygagging paid off. Halfway to the front doors and the street an idea struck. A gem!

Steinbrenner's timing couldn't have been better. Immediately upon walking in through the revolving door, he spotted a familiar black silk skirt trimmed with ruffles, a close-fitting basque coat with black velvet trimmed with ostrich feathers, and a bonnet of gray velvet trimmed with flowers. Brünnhilde stood at the front desk, talking to the clerk. Steinbrenner strode up to her and tapped her on the shoulder. She turned. Her reaction combined surprise, fear, and guilt. He had startled her so her hand went to her breast, and she leaned back against the desk for support.

"My dear, my dear." He seized her hand and kissed it.

"Gerhard," she murmured. Recovering swiftly, she turned to the clerk. "Never mind, thank you, this is the gentleman I was telling you about."

They walked toward the elevators.

"Where are your bags?" she asked.

"Back in Cheyenne, I regret to say. I will tell you all about it on the way up. Suffice it to say, if I had not had my wits about me, and my daring, I would not be here now."

"What happened?"

"Everything."

He detailed his experiences. They walked softly down the corridor to her door.

"Is your wound painful?" she asked.

"It was. And nearly fatal. An inch higher and the bullet would have passed through my heart."

"Dear me. And you say you lost the twenty thousand?"

"I did not 'lose' a thing," he said irritably. "That bastard Pinkerton, that ignorant yokel took it and everything else from me. I have barely thirty dollars left. Thank God for you, *Liebchen*. You *did* pull it off?"

"I . . . yes, of course."

He started at the sight of the suite when she unlocked and opened the door.

"*Mein Gott,* what splendor, what luxury! You certainly did not stint on accommodations, I see. How much?"

"Only twenty a week."

"Only, she says. It is lovely." He marched to the windows and stood with his hands clasped behind him, rocking on his heels, looking down on the traffic. Then he turned.

"So how did it go? Flawlessly? My dear, what is the matter?"

"Nothing."

"You seem nervous." He stiffened, touched his tongue to his upper lip, and hardened his stare. "Where's the money?"

"I have it."

"Good girl. Come come come."

She got the shoe box out from under the bed.

He fairly snatched it from her. "Twenties. All twenties," he muttered. Avarice set his eyes gleaming.

"Gerhard, there's something I must tell you."

"Is this the whole thirty thousand? It does not look like

that much," he asked without looking at her, his eyes riveted to the contents of the box.

"Gerhard, it's counterfeit."

Clutching two handfuls, he dropped the nearly empty box at his feet. He spread the money on the bed and began to count it.

"Counterfeit, I said."

"It looks more like twenty thousand. *Lieber Gott,* what cheap quality. The paper is like foolscap. Absolute trash. Americans have a lot to learn about paper money. They..."

He stopped. He went rigid.

"I brought our money to the bank in two separate trips. I exchanged it for this in the vault. Nobody saw, nobody suspected. It was so easy, so uncomplicated. It wasn't until Friday I found out *this* is counterfeit too. Mr. Hoffler told me. Sterling was long gone by then."

He turned slowly, mechanically, like a gypsy fortune-teller in a glass case in the penny arcade. His voice came from deep in his throat, a stunned and desperate rasping sound. "What are you babbling about?"

She explained, slowing her words. He sank down upon the bed. He listened, looking through her, letting it register blow by painful blow. He began to slowly shrink into himself under the steady punishment.

"Counterfeit."

"I never dreamed, I—"

"You imbecile! You bungling, stupid cow! You feeble-minded bitch! You exchanged our perfectly good tens for this? This junk! This trash!" He roared, jumped from the bed, and seized her by the throat. "I'll kill you!"

She jerked free and backed away. "Listen to me," she pleaded. "It wasn't my fault. He fooled us all: Hoffler, the other officers, everybody in the bank."

He lumbered after her, hands outstretched to grab her again. She was agile and too fast for him. Around the bed she sprinted, putting it between them.

"Control yourself! I can explain."

His growl died in his throat. His face had been redden-

ing fast, darkening, approaching purple; the veins in his ck
protruded like vines; his eyes thrust from their sockets like
a madman's; he worked his fingers, strangling the air; his
breath issued forth in short gasps, as if he were fighting for
air. He looked at her as if his brain was splitting in his
skull.

He stopped abruptly, straightened, dropped his hands to
his sides, sucked his lungs full, let it out slowly, and covered his face with his hands.

"Mein Gott!"

She took advantage of the sudden cessation of his anger
to complete her explanation. He sank into a chair, then
dropped his hands and gazed at her.

"You are *working* in the bank? A job?"

"That's what I'm trying to tell you. Instead of flirting
with a lovelorn teller, I changed my approach. I actually
got a job. My second try. No references, no friends to
vouch for me. The Crocker Bank. On Market Street."

"How far?"

"A leisurely walk from here."

"You work *inside* the vault? Where all the money is?"

"Most of the time. I have a small desk just outside the
door."

He had begun pacing, plunging into thought, breaking
out of it only to speak, pacing when she spoke, thinking,
but taking in her every word.

"Why did you take only twenties in exchange?"

"I guess because there seemed to be more twenties than
any other denomination."

"And that in itself did not arouse their suspicions?"

"No one noticed until Mr. Hoffler discovered they were
counterfeit. There was, as I said, two hundred thousand in
all. But slipped into the vault in small portions over a period of time, I'm sure."

"What is the matter with you? How could you be so
stupid? You should have exchanged for all different denominations. The totals at the end of the day would have
been the same, of course. And with you doing the
counting . . . Stupid cow!"

"I agree, it was thoughtless."

"Stupid!"

"Only, taking the twenties was easier and faster. And it seemed safe."

"Never mind alibiing."

"I'm not."

"Shut up, I am thinking. How much genuine have you left?"

"About a hundred and eighty."

"Out of four hundred? *Lieber Gott,* what did you do with it besides squander it on this Taj Mahal? Clothes, gourmet dinners? Never mind. Perhaps it is not a total loss after all. You did not quit your job . . ."

"No."

"Good. The one intelligent thing you seem to have done. So they do expect you at work tomorrow morning."

"What are you thinking?"

"I am thinking that with you having free access to the vault, handling money in full view of anyone there, permitted to, being paid to, this mess might be made to work out to our advantage after all."

The fear vanished from her tone. Her voice hardened perceptibly when she spoke. "You want me to rob the bank for you?"

"Do not be so gross, *Liebling,* so crass. You make it sound as if I want you to tie a handkerchief over your face and confront them with a revolver. I will devise something much more sophisticated that will not imperil you and that will bring us considerably more than thirty thousand. Oh my, yes." He clapped his hands sharply and rubbed them.

"I won't do it, Gerhard."

"You have not even heard my scheme."

"I don't want to. I wouldn't have the nerve. I'd go to pieces. I'd make a mess of it. They'd catch me."

"Shut up! You've already made a mess of it. A disaster. Out of the kindness of my heart I offer you a chance to make amends for your stupidity and you are afraid to try. Well, you will. And you will succeed. You will do as I tell you, understand? Or end up wishing you and I never met!"

"I already do!"

He slapped her.

She recoiled, putting her hand up to prevent a second slap. She glared defiantly.

Raider's plan, his gem, took only twenty minutes to execute. Emerging from the station, he walked straight to the first hansom cab in the long line at the curb and spoke to the driver. He described Steinbrenner's mustachios and asked if he had had such an individual for a fare today or yesterday. Cabs departed with their fares, others drew up at the end of the line prepared to pick people up. He worked his way slowly down the line, hopes high, pleased with himself, proud of his ingenuity.

Twenty-three drivers shook their heads when he described Steinbrenner. No fewer than a dozen remarked that they "sure would remember such a mustache." The twenty-fourth driver was an elderly wraith with alcoholic eyes and the breath to match. His hands resembled dead fish slipped out of his frayed cuffs. His right hand holding his whip shook visibly. He had but one tooth willing to display itself to the world. He drooled.

"Blond mustaches?" he croaked. "Hell yes."

"When?"

"Today. Round noon."

Raider described Steinbrenner in more detail.

"That's him."

"Where'd you take him?"

The man rubbed his chin with his free hand, crinkled his brow in thought, and drooled some more.

"Where?"

"I'm thinking, I'm thinking. I get forty, fifty fares a day; everybody going to a different place."

"A hotel. Which one? Think!"

"Hey, buddy," called a man standing with an old woman up the way. "You're holding up the parade."

A uniformed policeman turned his attention to the scene. Raider got the driver to move up a space to allow the cab behind him to pull out.

"You just lost me a fare, brother," the man complained.
You got a fare. Me. Which hotel?"

"Good question. There's so many of 'em."

"How much to jog your memory?" Raider got out a
seated Liberty half-dollar and held it up as anyone else
might a 50-carat diamond. "This help any?"

"Makes me sick is what it does," said the wraith.

"You're bein' greedy," said Raider, bowing his neck.

"You're being cheap. Why don't you just beat it?"

"How much, damn it!"

"Ten bucks'd make me feel lots better."

Raider felt flaring indignation, but kept control.
"Haven't got ten bucks. Matter o' fact, I'm just about
tapped out."

"How do you expect to pay for the ride?"

"I got three dollars and this fifty cents. I had more,
plenty more, but had to pay my train fare out from
Cheyenne. I was set on and robbed outside a bar back
there. Thief got away with my wallet. If I hadn't've had
some money stashed in my hind end pocket . . ."

"All right, all right. Jesus Christ, I don't believe a damn
word. Get in."

"Where to?"

"That's what *I'm* supposed to say. The Crocker House.
On Channel near Third. That's where I took him."

"Good! Great! Let's go!"

EIGHTEEN

While Raider was haggling with the cab driver a seemingly inauspicious event took place at the desk in the lobby of his destination. By the time he got there the desk clerk with whom Brünnhilde had been talking and who saw Steinbrenner arrive and come up to her went off duty and was replaced by a hawk-faced, middle-aged man whose expression hinted that he'd just finished sucking a sour grape.

Raider sprinted up to him. Head down, the clerk was busy going through the registration book.

"Hey fella, I've got an important question."

Without raising his eyes from the book, the clerk held up his hand.

"Important . . . Hey!"

The man jerked his head up and leveled an intimidating stare at him. "Right with you, sir!"

"Okay, okay. Shake it up, huh?"

After fully a minute, during which time Raider fidgeted, aimlessly tapped the desk with his index finger, straightened, cast about the lobby, returned his attention to the desk and the clerk, planted his elbows on the desk, removed his Stetson and set it down, again straightened and

171

drilled the clerk with his eyes, willing him to return his attention, the target of his impatience did so.

"Now what is so urgent?"

He described Steinbrenner. The man listened impatiently, then smirked in triumph as he shook his head. "No one like that has come in."

"You sure?"

"No one."

"He musta!"

"No one. I would have seen him, wouldn't I?"

"Not with your nose buried in that book, you wouldn't."

"See here!"

"He's gotta have come in. The cab that brought me here, the driver brought him before. Man swore up and down he did."

"He may have let him off in front, but no such individual came in."

"Well, how about the woman?" rasped Raider in desperation. "Pretty, I think. Dark hair, I think. Good build, well dressed."

"Is this some kind of joke? That description would fit a hundred ladies."

"She's registered. Gotta be!"

"Ah, now we're getting somewhere." He opened the book. "What name?"

"Ah . . . I dunno."

He closed the book. "We're not getting anywhere." He shifted his shoulders and looked past Raider. "May I help you, sir, madam?"

An oversized Texas-type—Raider could spot the boots and ten-gallon hat a half mile away—stepped up with a small blond bird attached to his arm. Raider stepped to one side as they registered. The clerk hammered the bell, the bellboy came running up, the two new arrivals followed him and their luggage to the elevator. Raider had not wasted time watching them; he put his mind to his problem. The clerk once again free and defenseless, he confronted him. "How long you been on?"

"Twenty minutes."

"Where's the boy whose place you took?"

"If you're referring to Orson Fellows, he is not a 'boy,' and he is off until eight tomorrow morning."

"Where'd he go?"

"I haven't the slightest idea."

"Boy, you sure as hell are a lotta help. Where could he've gone?"

An older, paternal-looking man with a pair of gold-rimmed spectacles poised awkwardly, dangerously close to the end of his nose, came over. "Anything wrong, Percival?"

"Nothin'," said Raider. "Except gettin' a straight answer outta Percival here. It's like pullin' nails with your teeth."

Pointedly ignoring his antagonist, Raider repeated Steinbrenner's description to the older man, who began to shake his head four words into Raider's speech.

"Whatta you shakin' no for? I haven' even hardly started, Chrissakes."

"Shh, please, this is the Crocker House."

"I know that. I . . ."

Raider stopped short. Across the lobby, just beyond an oak column, the elevator door opened and out stepped Steinbrenner and his accomplice. She looked harried, troubled; he looked as cocksure and unruffled as ever. Raider took one look and began backing away, circling backwards around a couple crossing in front of the desk, around an overstuffed chair, backing squarely into a second one, startling the occupant, turning and practically leaping behind a column. The two men behind the desk stood gaping, eyeing him as if he'd suddenly snapped. He noticed, waved, grinned sheepishly, and followed Steinbrenner and the woman out the door with his eyes. Then he ran across the lobby, waiting for the revolving door to come around, and pushed through it just in time to spy them rounding the corner into Third Street.

He stayed well behind them, letting a host of pedestrians come between, even to blocking out sight of them completely, keeping an eye on her pink and white parasol bobbing lightly above the crowd. The streets were mobbed. The parasol seemed to float under its own power above a multitude of heads.

They appeared to be heading toward the Embarcadero. The parasol rounded a corner, then another. The sidewalk continued crowded. Suddenly, his eyes glued to the parasol blinked and widened in surprise. An identical one appeared, coming from the opposite direction. A third showed across the street. His heart quickened. He bulled forward, dodging out into the gutter to get closer. Dodged an oncoming cab, narrowly missed knocking down two elderly women crossing the street, drawing the glare of a policeman directing traffic at the intersection.

"Faster!" hissed Steinbrenner.

"But if he's seen us, he'll notice and speed up too."

"He has seen us, you idiot, why else would he be following? Stop arguing at every word and do as you are told, damn it!"

"Gerhard . . ."

They rounded a corner, then another, and found themselves in a shadowed canyon between lofty warehouses. In marked contrast to Third and Howard, the street up and down was all but deserted. Past the third doorway on their right an alley led to a tall wooden fence at the distant end, barely discernible in the shadows.

"Down here. *Schnell!* We will crouch behind those refuse barrels. And put down that foolish parasol. You might as well be waving a flag at him! Why did you have to change from the black outfit? That dress sticks out like a torch!"

Raider ran and ran, turning into the now deserted street flanked by the towering warehouses. He stopped, looking up and down. He turned right, dashing past the alley, stopping thirty feet beyond and coming back. He squinted down it at the fence. It rose twenty feet; Steinbrenner couldn't possibly scale it even standing on a barrel, much less his companion.

He continued on, convinced they were hiding somewhere in the block. He had closed the gap close enough to spot them turning the corner behind him, and by the time he did, even running their fastest they would never have made it to the next block and around that corner.

He reached the corner, crossed, and started down the other side, checking every door. Every door was Sunday locked except one, the entrance to a large building displaying a gilt-on-black sign above the entrance: "Galbraith & Sons Merchant Marine Supplies & Equipment." He went in cautiously, quietly, gun drawn. The front office was small, archaic, and dusty. He tried the door at the back; it was locked. He glanced about. It was the only access to the warehouse proper. Evidently, whoever had been the last one to leave the night before had locked the interior door, paused to attend to one last thing, and, preoccupied with the task, had gone out and neglected to lock the street door.

He went back outside, crossed the street, and started down the other side a second time. Coming to the alley, he looked down it again and, drawing his gun, went down to investigate. It was empty, except for half a dozen trash barrels. In one he spied the parasol. The handle was snapped in two, as if broken over somebody's knee.

He cursed himself for his failure to search the alley the first time.

The Embarcadero is the street where the city meets the sea. In the freight yards, warehouses, and factories collected about the Southern Pacific depot it begins, running north, curving northwest and then west, encountering Market Street and the Ferry Building, bending again with the outward curve of the waterfront and heading westward to stop abruptly at Fisherman's Wharf amidst drying crab nets, fishing boats, rickety piers, hosts of sea birds, and squat little Italian restaurants.

In one such restaurant they sat in a booth at the rear drinking coffee as dark as pitch and plotting. Rather he plotted; she obligingly, obediently listened.

"You will go to work tomorrow morning as usual. On time. You will bring your lunch in a paper sack as you say you generally do, as most of the employees do. You will eat your lunch at your desk. Before closing time, just before, no more than five minutes before you leave for the day, you will remove a hundred thousand in mixed denominations from the vault. Large mixed denominations: hundreds, five hundreds. No twenties. Place them in your empty lunch sack and sneak it out in your handbag. When you leave the hotel tomorrow morning, check out. You will not be returning there. After we leave here now we will stroll up the dock and find us our ship."

"Gerhard . . ."

Up came his hand. "Do not interrupt."

"I must. Please listen. I cannot rob the bank. It is too dangerous."

"It is not at all. You are a trusted employee. No one will have any reason to suspect you when you leave with the money. No one will know it is missing until the next day. By then we will be on the high seas."

"You don't understand. Mr. Hoffler is on his guard. It was he who discovered the counterfeit twenties."

"So?"

"Our counterfeit tens, the whole thirty thousand, have been there almost a week now. They're being passed through the windows to the public just like the twenties were. His suspicions are aroused. He's probably at the bank this very minute examining *all* the money. He's sure to spot ours."

"Nonsense. He has been burned with the twenties; his whole attention is on them and the problem they've created. With his hands full of bogus twenties, why on earth would he examine any other denominations? What could possibly lead him to suspect a second counterfeiting scheme? You are being absurd. Not thinking as usual."

"It's too risky!"

"Shhhh, damn you."

"If I am caught, they will lock me up for twenty years."

"Come, come, *Liebchen*, what is this sudden timidity? These cold feet, as the Americans say? You have been in tight spots before. You know how to handle yourself. There is no danger, I tell you. Think! Use your head!"

"Shhhh, please."

"I repeat, no danger, absolutely none. Why? Because you will be on your own, not conspiring with some pathetic, lonely, frustrated, embittered teller. Yes, the shortage will be discovered. Unquestionably. But by then we will be miles from here."

He left off bullying and threatening and began to appeal to her, striving to convince her that everything he was saying made sense, that her fears of discovery were groundless. He appealed to her loyalty, citing their partnership, friendship, professing his love for her. Bridling his temper, he became more and more ardent.

"When the ship puts in, wherever we land, the first thing we will do is find a clergyman, a priest, and be married. That is what you want, *Liebchen*, no? Mr. and Mrs. Gerhard Steinbrenner."

"Mmmmm."

"And we will quit the business. No more jobs, no more traveling, no more Fenstermacher breathing down our necks. Of course now it is Raider; Fenstermacher is dead."

"How can you be sure of that?"

"I saw his corpse. He got to Cheyenne and promptly got into a barroom brawl and was shot to death."

"I don't believe it."

"I swear to you on my honor, on my love for you, it is God's truth. So you see, this last job will be our farewell to the business. It is time to get out. I have lost my press, all my equipment, practically all my money. I see it as a sign, a warning from the Fates. It is time to retire. That is what you want?"

She sighed heavily, finished her coffee, and set the cup down. "You do love me, don't you?" Her tone very nearly implored.

"With all my heart and soul. Does not the fact that from the day that we met I have not so much as looked at another woman prove it? I worship you, Brünnhilde."

"Let's go back to the hotel." Her dark, luminous eyes glowed yearningly.

"No. *That* is too risky. Raider is probably already back there, waiting for us to return. On second thought, we will not go back at all."

"But my things, my clothes, my jewels."

"Neither of us. Come, let us go and make arrangements for our passage. We can sleep on board tonight. Stay clear of the hotel. The city proper. Tomorrow you will go to work, do what you have to do, leave there, come directly to the ship. I will be waiting, and within the hour we will sail away."

NINETEEN

Having lost sight of his quarry, Raider stopped to sort out the situation. He came up with four assumptions. He decided that, having spotted them in the Crocker House lobby, they would not go back there under any circumstances. He decided that from now on they would stick together; breaking up to keep him off the track didn't make sense. Decided that when they were certain they'd shaken him off they would head for the dock to find a ship. And decided they would leave on the first vessel out.

He had no way of knowing, but in three of the four he was right. Had no way of knowing that Brünnhilde was virtually as broke as Steinbrenner and that it would be necessary for them to delay their departure for one day at least. Further, Raider was unaware that in her week in San Francisco she had become a trusted employee of the Crocker Bank.

He returned to Market Street and walked down it to within sight of the bay. Around the peninsula's edge, from Fisherman's Wharf to China Basin, swept the 200-foot-wide Embarcadero. Where the four-masters and square-riggers had set sail from over the past century, now only three sailing vessels bobbed at anchor, vastly outnumbered by smoke-belching steamers. The smells of copra, of raw sugar, roasting coffee, and rotting piles and mud and salt permeated the area.

He hesitated to show himself, reasoning that if he was right, if they were in the area, they would spot him all too easily. He briefly considered disposing of his Stetson, a dead giveaway among so many derbies and various other "city" hats, but told himself he should have thought of that before they stepped out of the elevator. That had to be where Steinbrenner spotted him, notwithstanding his efforts to stay out of sight.

All the downtown streets ended at the Embarcadero. He walked back up Washington and stopped two sailors heading in the direction he had come from.

"You boys know where the harbormaster's office is?"

They sent him to the sprawling Ferry Building. In front of it he got further directions to the harbormaster's office, along with a reminder that it was Sunday and the office was closed. He grumbled his thanks and wandered off. Keeping to the shadows on the city side of the Embarcadero, he walked almost its entire length counting oceangoing vessels. To his dismay there were nearly a hundred. Still, he reasoned, all of them couldn't be leaving tonight. He thought briefly of returning to the Ferry Building and the harbormaster's, breaking in, and looking for the arrival-departure book, whatever they called it, and pinning down which specific ships would be leaving. But if he was caught breaking and entering . . .

"They'd fry my hide, tie me up in red friggin' tape, telegrams back and forth to Chicago. Steinbrenner'd get away for sure."

He could see no alternative but to hang around the docks, hoping and praying, but in his heart willing to give long odds against spotting them. He was wrong. An hour later, as the sun began to lower over the city at his back, he was standing on the corner of Battery Street and Lombard, studying five vessels in line, moored side by side. On the foredeck of the fourth one, its name hidden by the prow of the third, three figures appeared. The master of the vessel was easy to identify. Just as easy was Steinbrenner. And her dress perfectly matched her broken and discarded parosol.

"Lady Luck, I love you," he murmured.

He slipped around the corner of the nearest building, then carefully edged partially back out to confirm his discovery. The captain leaned on the railing, smoking his pipe and waving goodbye. Steinbrenner followed her down the gangplank.

He checked his gun. It was now or probably never, he thought. He had lost him three times, found him three times; losing him a fourth would be stretching his luck too far. He watched them linger at the foot of the gangplank, then start away. They were coming toward him, walking slowly down the sea side of the Embarcadero. When they got directly opposite him, they would be almost exactly two hundred feet away.

Closer and closer they came. Gun up, he backed against the building as they passed. Both had their heads down. They appeared to be arguing. She seemed to be more upset than he. He gestured in a manner that suggested he was appealing to her, trying to convince her of something.

Raider let them get about half a block past, then started across the street after them. He got all the way across without either of them turning to look back. They were now a block and a half ahead. He broke into a run.

Steinbrenner heard. He turned and recognized him.

"Get 'em up!"

Both had stopped. She looked horrified. Steinbrenner started to raise his hands, stopped halfway up, grabbed her, pulled her in front of him, jerked out his gun. The second he grabbed her Raider fired. Steinbrenner's first two shots zipped by perilously close. He crouched behind her. Raider gasped. She screamed. Raider's shot struck her in the chest. She went limp. Raider had dropped flat. Deprived of his shield, Steinbrenner did not fire a third time; he turned and ran. Up on his feet Raider took off after him. He ran and ran, past her prostrate form, out onto the dock, caught

sight of him, lost him, glimpsed him, and began to close
the gap. Steinbrenner sent a worried look back over his
shoulder, turned, and fired on the run. Wildly. Three shots.
None of which came close. Raider held his fire.

Steinbrenner glanced back and fired a fourth shot, a
fifth. Tried to. His weapon clicked harmlessly. He panicked, veering sharp right, running out onto a wharf. By
the time Raider reached it and turned to follow, he was
almost to the end, with no place to go but into the sea
softly lapping at the piles.

As Raider pulled up and raised to fire, Steinbrenner
slipped behind a pile butt, dropping from sight. Raider
rushed forward. If he could get to him before he could
reload . . . He did not. He was not ten strides toward him
before man and gun reappeared; two hurried shots came
winging at him. Wild. Missing.

Raider threw himself behind a pile. Steinbrenner had
obviously, shrewdly, reloaded only two chambers. Now he
was full-loading. Raider jumped from his concealment,
sprinting to the next pile in line, closing the distance sepa-
rating them to less than twenty yards. He crouched and
waited.

"Raider! Raider! I know you can hear. Listen, I can
make you a rich man. Enough money to last you a lifetime.
Put it back in your holster and let me walk by you. We will
go back to the hotel. I will give you fifty thousand. Cash.
Genuine. If that is not enough . . . Raider?"

Silence.

Raider waited fully two minutes. Then sneaked a peek.
Two shots came blasting, missing, but too close. He returned one. He reloaded the two emptied chambers, then
looked to his left down over the edge at the murky water
below. The wharf was so constructed that if he dropped
down over the edge he could move forward toward him
hand over hand. But he'd be a goner if Steinbrenner heard
him and looked down. He'd have to drop into the water.
He'd be a sitting duck. When he surfaced he'd catch one
dead-bang in the head.

"Forget it."

Again Steinbrenner fired, showing only hand and forearm. Raider did not answer. He waited. A third time Steinbrenner fired. Ready and waiting, almost the instant he got his shot off, Raider returned. A scream—loud, high-pitched like a woman. A clattering. He looked out. He'd hit him in the hand or wrist. Down on all fours, Steinbrenner scrambled to retrieve his gun.

Raider jumped to his feet. "Hold it right there!"

On his knees, his gun within reach, Steinbrenner froze. He raised his hands and got to his feet.

"My hand . . ."

Blood glistened down his right hand under his index finger. A scratch. Raider kicked his gun into the water.

"Let's go, you son of a bitch."

He did not budge. Disgust seized his handsome face. "You murdered her in cold blood. A woman. How could you?"

"You're the one murdered her, pullin' her in front o' you."

"Filthy, murdering swine!"

Raider growled, glared, hauled off and with his free fist, knocked him flat and cold. His shoulder exploded with pain. He stood gritting his teeth, sweating it away. Then bending over, slapped him back to consciousness. He ordered him to his feet and marched him back to the dock. A crowd had gathered around the body.

Steinbrenner took one look, cried out, covered his face with his hands, and began to sob bitterly.

TWENTY

William Wagner sat at his desk in his shirtsleeves and vest puffing on a La Mathilde cigar and discussing the case with Raider, who was sitting opposite him behind a cigar of his own.

"Steinbrenner's on his way back to Germany, as well as Fenstermacher's body and the woman's, too."

"Whatta ya think he'll get?"

"Nice, comfortable noose."

"Couldn't happen to a nicer fella."

"You did a fine job under rough circumstances, Rade. But then, don't you always."

"Ah . . ."

"Say, I almost forgot, this came in for you just before you got here. From Washington. The chief's there at the invitation of Secretary of State Evarts. Something big and hush hush."

He scaled a sealed telegram across the desk. Raider caught it and read it to himself.

CONGRATULATIONS WRAPUP CASE STOP SHAME COULD NOT ACCOMPLISH SAME EARLIER AND

185

> THEREBY SAVE LIVES TWO GERMANS STOP ALSO
> MUST TAKE ISSUE WITH YOUR FAILURE TO SEND
> BACK PERIODIC REPORTS STOP HAD YOU DONE
> SO YOUR FAILURE TO RECEIVE OUR WIRE
> ALERTING YOU SUSPECTS TRUE IDENTITY
> WOULD HAVE PREVENTED AFOREMENTIONED
> DEATHS STOP GENERAL PRINCIPLES TO BE OB-
> SERVED AND OBEYED STOP IN ADDITION
> DEATHS OF FARMER AND WIFE COULD HAVE
> BEEN AVOIDED

"Oh for Chrissakes, I don't have to read this crap, this bitchin' an' carpin'. All he does is find fault. Never a damn kind word, never 'Thank you, Raider, good job well done.' Pick nit an' nitpick is all he can ever do. Man makes me sick to pukin'!"

As he ranted and reddened his stubbled face Wagner got a letter out of the pocket of his jacket, which was draped over the back of his chair.

"Rade . . ."

"I could be lyin' back there dead as a stump, and he wouldn't care. Damn rattler's got more human feelin's than him!"

"Rade . . ."

"What?"

"He sent me this. Listen." He mumbled through the first few lines. "Here it is. 'Regarding Cheyenne case Raider completed in San Francisco, Will, the lad never ceases to amaze. Every new assignment he outdoes himself, outperforms his previous heroics. The man is a jewel, not only our top operative, but the shrewdest, most reliable, most courageous and tenacious I have ever known. If we ever decide to pass out awards for successes for going above and beyond the call of duty, he'll be the first recipient. None of the other boys can hold a candle to him. Will, when Pinkerton history is made, it's Raider who makes it, bless him. P.S. Don't mention this to him. Show this to no one else and destroy it after you read it.'

"What do you think of that?"

"Smoke. Bull. There's praisin' bull as well as criticizin' bull, you know. He's A-number-one at both. Anythin' in there about a raise? Read it again. Better yet, give it here. Let me. Must be somethin' about a raise. I'll hang on to it, throw it back at him when he comes back. Meantime I'll waltz it on over to the Illinois Commercial Bank, wake up Weatherbee at his desk, an' show it to him. Give it here."

Wagner refused. Raider sprang at him to seize it. Wagner jumped from his chair and ran out into the hall.

Raider sprinted after him. "Gimme the damn thing!"